# WINNER'S CREED

# WINNER'S CREED

BRENDA LEIGH

Primix Publishing
11620 Wilshire Blvd
Suite 900, West Wilshire Center, Los Angeles, CA, 90025
www.primixpublishing.com
Phone: 1-800-538-5788



Published by Primix Publishing    04/24/2023

ISBN: 979-8-88703-219-1(sc)
ISBN: 979-8-88703-220-7(e)

Library of Congress Control Number: 2023907162

# 1

**"Y**es!" Christy Rivers pumped her fist in the air as the ball dropped through the net with a soft swish.

*Eighty-nine out of ninety-nine.* A spontaneous smile broke through as she raced to catch the ball before dribbling one more time to the foul line. *With one more free throw, I would make the best percentage since deciding to shoot a hundred free throws a day.*

She wiped sweat from her eyes before focusing her attention on the goal in the center of the backboard. Raising the ball into a shooting position, she took a deep breath, concentrating on the shot. As soon as the ball left her hand, she knew it was going in.

"Yes! Yes! Yes!" She exclaimed joyfully once more as the ball dropped through the net.

Dancing across the concrete, she retrieved the ball, moving with a grace that she is unaware of. She bounced the ball toward the top of the key, loving the way the leather felt as it slapped against the palm of her hand.

The idea to become a better shooter began after hearing Liz Parker, the star player of the Lady Lions, tell everyone that she would never be more than a team manager. The first step had been turning the driveway at her home into a basketball court. The foul line with the rest of the lines had taken hours to paint, but the hours spent there were finally paying off.

The impish grin appeared again as she thought about practice the next day. No one was going to be able to say she couldn't shoot. At five-foot-four, what she lacked in height was made up for with an outside shot that was sure to change her chances of playing on the team. This was her senior year, making it her last chance to be a Lady Lion.

"Ninety out of a hundred free throws."

A laugh escaped from her lips. She had made eight out of a hundred the first time back in the middle of March. Just the thought of the looks on her teammates' faces again added a sparkle to her eyes.

She thought again about Liz. At one time, they had been good friends. But Liz had changed overnight. One day they were friends, and the next, she wouldn't even acknowledge her. Most of the change had begun when Liz became good at basketball and had little time for anything else. The past year, she had seemed to enjoy making life miserable for anyone who wasn't in her group of friends.

Liz and her new best friend, Sherri, had ruled the basketball court, deliberately keeping the ball from players that they didn't want on the team. They made passes they couldn't catch, tripped up players, and made life miserable enough that some gave up and quit. They were cool with their tactics, and Coach Johnson didn't seem to notice.

But to be fair, Christy knew her short stature and poor shooting skills had eliminated her from playing on the team the past two years. She was thankful Coach Johnson had allowed her to continue to work out with the team and be one of the managers. Playing on and being part of a team was something she had not given up on. Over the last few months anyone watching her practice would have thought she was training for the Olympics. She was up early working out because it was so hot later in the day. During that time, her determination grew stronger as each day she became better at free throws. She could now hit an outside jump shot her brother, Sam, had taught her the last time he was home on leave from the military. Now it was possible she would finally get to wear the Lady Lions' uniform that had been so elusive.

Since Liz didn't seem to like her, Christy knew being on the team might be a problem for Liz and some of her friends. As the leader of the team, Liz's had a lot of influence on how the other players would treat her. No matter the problems ahead, she was determined to keep a positive attitude for this year to be different.

With the basketball under her arm, Christy crossed toward the back door. Pausing near the door, she looked up to see her mother standing there with a bottle of cold water in one hand and shading her eyes from the sun with the other.

"Was it my imagination, or was your shooting really on today?"

"It was on. I made ninety percent of my free throws. Ninety out of one hundred --a vast improvement from where I started."

"That is wonderful!" Her mother laughed. "I thought I saw a little celebrating. You have about thirty minutes before dinner is ready if you want to get a shower."

"Okay, I think I will sit here and cool down a little first while I drink my water."

The heat of the hot August afternoon had Christy leaning back in her chair exhausted, but the drained feeling was going to be worth it. She pushed her dark-brown hair back from her face and placed the cold bottle against her cheeks. The temperature change caused her to catch her breath, but it felt so good. She closed her eyes and rested her head back on the chair cushion for a moment before slowly opening her eyes and gazing up at the sky.

"Thank You, Lord. Without You, none of this would be possible. I come with a thankful heart for all Your blessing in my life."

She believed God had helped her each step of the way --- in coming up with a plan, helping her stay focused on her goal to play, and letting her practice each day since setting that goal.

"I know You're busy up there with all the bad stuff that is going on in the world, but please continue to watch over Dad and Sam. Our soldiers need You to keep them safe as they face the dangers of their job. I worry especially about Sam. He is only twenty, and this is his second tour in a war zone. It all seems so unfair. Sometime when I listen to the news, and people are more concerned with mean and petty behavior toward each other than caring about one another. I don't understand the intolerable behavior of so many people in our country, Lord. Please help our nation to unify and work on getting their acts together, to care about each other again, to remember who You are, Lord. Help me to live a life that will always be pleasing to You, and draw me closer to You. Thanks for listening and for keeping my dad, brother, and America safe. Amen."

She let the peaceful reassurance that always followed a talk with God wash over her. A lot of people would say there was no God, but she had never let others influence her belief of what she felt in her heart as well as in her head. She felt bless that she had parents and grandparents who had taught her from an early age about God. Once she accepted Jesus as her Savior at twelve, she had promised to always take a stand for Him and not let others make her feel ashamed for her belief. Knowing many of her classmates, including Liz, called her "Jesus Chick" didn't upset her. It only made her all the more determined to live so others could see there was something different about her life.

Finishing her drink, she stood and headed for the back door, the cool air hit her in the face when she stepped inside. Her mother was at the cabinet, peeling the shell from boiled eggs and dicing them into a small side dish for a salad. Looking up, she rinsed her hands under the running water at the sink and dried them on a dish towel.

"You had better hurry. Gran should be here shortly, and I know she will be ready to eat."

"I'll hurry." Christy placed her water bottle in the recycle bin near the back door before heading for the hallway and the stairs.

Voices were coming from the kitchen as Christy left her room to go downstairs a short time later. They were laughing about something her Grandmother had said when she came through the door into the kitchen.

"Hi Gran." She went over to hug the silver hair woman.

Carrie Rivers was the same height as Christy, and their eyes were the same shade of blue. Anyone seeing them together would know where Christy got her beautiful eyes.

"I understand that your shooting was very good today," Gran said with a gleam in her eye. "I knew you could do it. I have never seen anyone work so hard and with so much determination."

"Tomorrow's the first day of practice, and I can't wait to see the look on Liz's and Sherri's faces when the shooting starts."

"They will be a little surprised along with the rest of the players and your coach. I have no doubt. I am so glad that you never gave up on your dream. You do know that's what made the difference and is most important."

"The turning point for me was when you talked about what God said about having the faith of a mustard seed, Gran. When you gave me that book marker showing me just how small a mustard seed was, that was when I knew I could do it."

"Just remember that it isn't the believing alone but putting that belief into action that counts. Without action, nothing is going to change. I may want to write a book and might even have the faith to do so, but if I never write any words down…"

"I know if I had just continued to do what I had in the past, nothing would have been any different this year.

Now I have a good chance of making the team and being able to see some playing time. Make sure to save some time for a few of our games this year."

"For sure." Gran smiled. "There is a poem that I wish I could remember all the words to. I had a bookmark of it once. I think the name was 'A Winner's Creed'. It fits in with what you are doing, and it talks about keeping faith and working hard while trusting God to help see you through. I will see if I can find another bookmark for you."

"Thanks, Gran," Christy said. "I would like that."

"Christy, if you will put ice in glasses and take care of the tea, I think dinner is ready," her mother told her as she took a casserole out of the oven and placed it on top of the stove to cool. The salad was ready on the cabinet.

Christy walked over to the cabinet and took out three glasses before moving over to the refrigerator for ice. Pouring tea into the glasses, she quickly placed a glass beside each place setting on the table. She took a salad bowl and fixed her salad and her plate before taking her seat at the table.

Once everyone was seated, they joined hands and bowed heads as her grandmother said grace. "Thank You, Lord, for this day and for each person here. We especially thank You for the food we are about to eat and for Mary who has worked so hard in preparing it. Lord, thank You for watching over our loved ones while they are away, and we pray You will continue to protect and keep them safe. Amen"

"How was your day?" Christy asked her grandmother.

"It was very entertaining. I met with the press and then Channel 7 News for the interview that was on the morning show. Then I went to the book signing at Barnes and Nobles off Chenal."

"I recorded the news program so we can all watch it together later. Your stand on the moral issues that are attacking our faith was right on," Mary commented. "You did a really good job by the way you handled the questions and gave verses in the *Bible* that backed up what you were saying. I think your book will help a lot of people."

"The attacks on our faith have been going on for years. Most of the questions I was expecting; only a few were new."

As a war correspondence, Christy's grandmother had written on many controversial issues over the years. Now in her retirement, she continued to write for several magazines and newspapers around the country. The morning interview was about a devotional book she was releasing and on concerns about political issues facing the Christian faith.

"I will admit that I got a little heated over one of the reporter's stands on the protesters at military funerals and how the Supreme Court ruling supports them."

"I remember that part of the interview but thought your answer was more in line with what God would expect of us. Quite frankly I can't believe people are willing to go that far to get attention," Mary said. "It stills has to be one of the cruelest things I have ever heard an American do for one of our own who has paid with their life fighting for this country when those poor families are dealing with the death of their loved one and adding to their pain. It just breaks my heart."

"I know that group won the Supreme Court decision

supporting their rights to protest, but what about the right the families have to bury a loved one without having to listen to their hateful remarks?" Christy asked. "I have seen them on TV, and some are really young, flashing signs that read "God Hates You" and "Thank God for Dead Soldiers" Using innocent children to deliver such a message of hatred while mocking and taunting grieving families is just un-American!"

"They do it to get attention for their message," Gran said. "They call it expressing their freedom of speech using their first amendment rights. They should just say the more outrageous I can be, the more likely you will give me your attention."

"They're so mean spirited with how they are going about it," Christy declared. "Why would anyone listen to them spew their hatred?" She paused for a moment, looking at both her mother and grandmother. "I just don't understand why people are so mean to each other and why they would enjoy taunting grieving families?"

"I don't know honey," Gran said. "When God gave mankind the freedom to make decisions, all the rest followed."

"How do we prevent that group from protesting at soldiers' funerals here?"

"Technically we don't. The first amendment gives them the right to protest," Gran answered. "Their actions aren't really any different than those made by many people during other wars. I remember when I was just a girl during the Vietnam War. We had lots of people protesting the war, and some families were treated badly at that time too."

"I remember one Sunday morning there was a funeral for a young soldier during the morning service in our little country cemetery. The preacher had the curtains pulled and acted like they should not be interfering with his sermon. I can still remember seeing people gather around a flag-draped coffin before the curtains were closed. A few of the older men went outside, but most people just sit there. I couldn't tell you one thing that preacher said that morning, but to this day I can still hear the twenty-one gun salute and the beautiful 'Taps' being played. It wasn't until years later that I fully understood the significance of what had taken place that morning. The price that young man paid still leaves me with sadness and regrets for that grieving family. Can you imagine what it would have meant to his family if that congregation had just gathered around them that morning and loved and prayed for them? Instead they missed out on a blessing, and I know they must have disappointed God."

"How sad, but you were just a young girl then and really didn't understand," Christy said.

"Yes, and sadly many of those children you see with those signs are just as innocent." Sadness was plain on her grandmother's face.

Compassion flooded Christy's heart for her grandmother as a young girl and for the group who did not understand they should care for their fellow man, especially for those who gave their life to keep them free. She couldn't help but wonder if the children in the middle of the protesters' group would one day understand the truth. *Or would they be just like the adults who were teaching them such hatred? Would they grow up to be just like them?*

"Some people do care, Gran. I know some states have tried to put laws in place where they can't protest within so many feet of where the funeral is taking place, and a few have even set times so many minutes before or after a funeral, so they are not there at the same time as these families. In many places, veterans and motorcycle riders have started setting up outside funerals to shield families."

"I know your right, honey," Gran replied. "I remember this happening in Cabot recently when an Arkansas soldier was killed. These riders were showing the respect they know these men and women deserve."

"All I can say about this group, is they had better not come here." Christy declared with heartfelt conviction.

"Don't even go there, dear," Gran replied. "No matter how much you hate what they are doing; hatred is what has us in a war to start with. Spreading more hatred is not the answer and never will be."

"I know, but they say they are a church." Christy's tone implied she couldn't believe it.

"Let it go and let the Lord deal with it, honey," Gran added. "There are too many other important issues in our world to be concerned with."

"All I can say is laws made by man are certainly not what I think God had in mind."

"Christy, just remember God's laws have not changed. They are still the same as they were when they were given years ago, and they will still be the same in the future, no matter how many laws are passed or changed to suit the changing lifestyle of a society. People feel they have the right to do as they please and forget there are consequences for doing so."

"There are so many people who don't believe in God, and they certainly don't want to hear about Him." Christy sadly admitted. "They talk badly about us because we want to share Jesus with others. Most of them will take anything they hear on the news or read on the internet as true but will not pick up a *Bible* to see what truth really is."

"I know, but do not get discouraged. Continue to tell others the good news. That's what God's Word says to do. That is what I said just this morning in the interview. This country is in need of some old-fashioned moral leadership based on what this country was founded on. We need to stop listening to the lies our society is telling us and pick up our *Bibles* and search the scriptures for how we should live and abide by the principles of God. Everyone is always wanting change for our country. I can only imagine what it could be like if we did turn back to God."

"What do you think your dad would say about all of this?" Christy's mother asked.

One of her father's favorite sayings came to her mind. "He would say when you are unsure of something, get out your *Bible* and read until your mind is clear on what the right thing to do is and then do it. His favorite quote was, "It is never wrong to do right, and it is never right to do wrong.""

"That is so true." Her mother replied.

"He would also say love God, love one another, and don't forget to pray for our country," Christy added.

"He would certainly add to pray for this group," her mother said.

"God's Word also says judge not that you be not judged?" Christy commented.

"Matthew 7," Gran said with a smile. "I daresay, if we all would spend a little more time in the Word of God, we would have a better view of the life we should be living and the message we should be spreading. What we really need to do is pray for all the young lives that are being influenced by the new morality bombarding our TVs and social media sites so commonly accepted by the world today."

"Gran, just so you know my compass is right where it needs to be because of you, Grandpa, Mom, and Dad. I have a firm foundation of how to live my life. I know God, He is my hope and is in my heart, and I plan to be true to Him all the days of my life."

"Never once will you ever walk along as long as you keep Him first, dear." Her mother hugged her as they rose from the table to take the dishes to the kitchen.

"There will be trials ahead, my dear. Just because you know the Lord doesn't mean bad things can't happen to you, but when you have God, you never face anything that He can't see you through."

"I know, Gran."

"Why don't you get ready to play that new song you have been practicing while your grandmother and I take care of these dishes?" Her mother asked.

"Gran you are going to love this song. It is such a great praise song. It is on Matt Redman's CD, *10,000 Reasons*, and was written by him and Jonas Myrin. We sing '10,000 Reasons' all the time, but this song is really special."

Christy sat down at the piano and ran her fingers over the keys to warm up before getting out her music for the song called "Magnificent." Each time she heard the song, she lost herself in the lyrics. Playing through the music, she let her fingers fly over the keys, silently singing the words in her mind. The second time through she sang just the chores. The next time through, she sang all of it, singing praises to her Lord and feels blessed to be able to worship Him in this way.

"You are Magnificent… You alone are Holy… No one else as glorious as You… Magnificent…  Jesus, You are worthy…" With eyes closed, she let the music fill her soul and felt closeness to the one she sang praises to. As the song ended, she opens her eyes to find both her mother and grandmother smiling at her.

"You were right, honey. It was magnificent. I love the way you sang it." Carrie Rivers came over to give her granddaughter a hug with tears in her eyes. "May you always love the Lord and keep your eyes on Him. Please continue singing and telling others about God's amazing grace and how it leads to salvation. People need to know that all they need to do to be saved is to confess with their mouth 'Jesus is Lord' and believe with their hearts that He died for their sins. If they ask Him to forgive their sins and come into their hearts, He will."

"It's amazing how much God loves us." Christy replied. "Sometimes I want to cry when people turn away with no interest in what He did for us."

"Don't give up, honey. Just keep praying for them. You may never know exactly the impact you might have on someone else. God does."

*Thank You, Lord, for those in my life who continue to help me to grow in knowledge of You and encourage me on this journey. As this school year begins, Lord, I ask You to lead and guide me to always give my best and to do Your will. I want to be a girl after Your heart, Lord, and to live my life on Your terms. I Love You*

# 2

Bounding down the stairs, Christy felt excited that the first day of basketball practice was finally here. The petite figure moved energetically, her canvas tennis shoes making little sound on the wood steps. Pausing on the bottom step, she pushed dark-brown hair away from her face when she heard sobs coming from the direction of her mother's bedroom down the hallway to her left.

Even before reaching the entrance to her mother's room, she knew something was terribly wrong. Her mother hardly ever cried and certainly not like she was now. She felt her heartbeat accelerate when she saw her mother sitting on the side of the bed with tears rolling down her face and could only think it was probably something to do with her dad or brother.

"Please, Lord, don't let it be Dad or Sam," she whispered under her breath, hating the fear she felt as she crossed the room to her mother's side.

Christy's blue eyes were drawn to the TV screen where

a news announcer was saying, "Two servicemen were killed overnight by an IED." The men were obviously from the Arkansas guard unit her father and brother were stationed with.

"Mom!" she exclaimed, fear evident in her voice.

"It's not Dad or Sam," her mother was able to whisper between sobs. "Give me a moment."

Christy put her arms around her mother and sat on the side of the bed. After a few moments, her mother became quieter. Taking her mother's hand, she began to pray, "Dear heavenly Father, we need Your loving care at this time. We know You know our needs before we ask, and we just ask that You will be with Dad, Sam and all the members of their unit that need your care and protection at this moment. Please be with the families that have lost loved ones, and may Your tender mercy be with each one. May this terrible war soon be over, and all of our loved ones return safely home. Be with us and give us the strength we need to face the day. We love You, Lord. Amen."

Mary raised her head and reached for a tissue from the nightstand beside the bed. "Please forgive me, honey, I didn't mean to fall apart like that. I heard about the soldiers earlier and have been on the phone trying to find out something. I'm afraid Ben Masters was one of the soldiers killed, but I don't know the other soldier except that he was a young man with your dad's unit.

"Oh, Mom, that's Sarah's dad." Christy cried tears in her eyes for her friend that she had met at church camp the past summer. Sarah and her family lived in Hot Springs, but they had family that lived near Wilmot.

"I know, honey. It was just so unexpected when I

first heard about it this morning, and for a little while, I thought it might be your dad or Sam. Ben Masters is also Jenny Reynold's uncle. I was able to reach one of the people that your dad gave me to call and was able to find out it wasn't Dad or Sam. Little information was available for release until the next of kin were notified. They just said the names a few minutes ago, so I guess the families must know by now."

"It's alright, Mom. I understand." Christy knew she had experienced the same frightening experience many times in the last few months. The war was taking its toll on lots of families around the country as it continued on and on. Lately she had noticed that the pressure was really beginning to age her mother, and she always looked so sad. "Do you want me to call Gran to come over for a while before I go to school?"

The tears had stopped, and the gentle smile returned to her mother's face. "No, I'm okay now. I just have to keep reminding myself God is in control and I have to trust him with all of this."

"That's what Dad would say. Thanks, Mom, for being such a good teacher. You and Dad both have been great examples in your teaching Sam and me about God."

"Your dad and I made a commitment to God that we would raise our children in a godly household like we were raised." A wistful look appeared on her face as she picked up the picture of her family that she kept on the nightstand beside her bed. Touching her husband's face, she smiled again. "It seemed only yesterday we were bringing you home."

"Now I am a senior in high school who is going to be

late on her second day of school if I don't hurry." Christy looked at her wristwatch.

"Heaven! Is that the time?" Mary asked. "I need to fix you some breakfast."

"Don't worry about me I will find something."

Christy found it hard to leave her mother, but she walked to the kitchen for a bowl of cereal before going back upstairs to finish getting ready for school. Coming down the stairs to get her notebook and purse a few minutes later, she couldn't just walk out without knowing her mom was okay. Taking a detour, she walked back to the door of her mother's room, but she had her *Bible* open and her head down. She seems calm now, so Christy decided she could go.

Going through the laundry room to the garage, she opened the garage door from the inside before putting her things into the jeep. She liked driving the jeep that belonged to Sam while the weather was still warm and she didn't have to worry about having the top on. She backed the jeep out and pushed the button on the garage opener so the door closed until her mother wanted it open later in the day.

She smiled as she thought of Sam and how much he loved the jeep when he had gotten it for graduation two years earlier. Unfortunately, he'd had little time to drive it before going to basic training, and shortly after that, he was in the middle of a war zone in Iraq. On his last visit home, he had told her to drive it her senior year and break it in for him. Now he was in Afghanistan with her father's unit for a second tour of duty. He was only twenty years old, and it seemed so unfair that he was serving his country in a war that most people didn't seem to care about.

The crisp morning air felt good on her skin as she made the drive to school. It lifted her dark-brown hair, blowing it about, but she didn't mind. She could run a hairbrush through it when she arrived at school. As she listened to the familiar words from a worship song, her fingers tapped out the rhythm as she let the message roll over her. The short five-mile trip didn't take long, but as she neared the school, traffic caused her to slow down and keep her mind on her driving.

She pulled into her parking space on the high school campus and had just put the jeep in park and turned the engine off when her two best friends, Karri Taylor and Anne Wilson, rushed up to her. As she lingered in the jeep for a few moments to run a brush through her hair her eyes fell on her friends.

"Where have you been? We thought we were going to have to send out a search party," Anne explained.

"Sorry! I'm running a little late," Christy replied not really wanting to talk about why she was.

"You'll never guess what has happened!" Karri added.

"What?" She slammed the jeep door after picking up her notebook and purse.

"She definitely hasn't heard." Karri told Anne.

"Heard what?" Christy's expression showed bewilderment as she looked at the happy expressions on her two friends' faces.

"About Coach Johnson." Anne said.

"Hey, wait up!" Tonya Cook, a tall African American

girl, called as she rushed up to join their group. "You will never believe what happened to me this summer."

"Hey Tonya," Christy was the first to greet her. "Karri and Anne were about to tell me some news about Coach Johnson."

"She took Liz and me to the Lady Razorbacks basketball camp in July," Tonya told them. "Wait till you see some of my new moves when we get on the court today."

"Sounds like you had a good camp," replied Karri.

"I meet so many of the Razorback players. I got several players' autographs." She laughed. "The only bad thing was being at camp the entire week with Liz." She rolled her eyes at them, and all three girls laughed together without having to ask for details.

"Now what is the news about Coach Johnson?" Christy prompted once more directing the conversation back to their basketball coach.

"She isn't coaching this year." Karri answered.

"You're kidding right?" Tonya replied, obviously as shocked by the news as Christy. "Oh man, I can't believe this! And just when I finally get her attention, she's leaving us."

"Why?" Christy questioned as she looked up and saw Jenny Reynolds just a short distance away from where they stood. "What is Jenny doing here?"

"Last I heard, she goes to school here," Karri responded.

"That's not what I meant," she replied. "I didn't expect to see her at school today. There was some information on her uncle on the news. Do you think she knows?"

"What news?" Karri questioned as Christy left their

group and began walking over to where Jenny stood talking to another girl.

"Jenny are you okay?" Christy asked as she met Jenny's eyes.

"Why wouldn't I be?" she asked.

"You didn't hear the news this morning?" Christy said, knowing at that moment that Jenny had no idea what she was talking about just by the bewildered look on her face.

"N-no." Jenny shook her head. "Why? What is wrong?"

"Your Uncle," Christy paused because she couldn't just tell Jenny her uncle was dead.

"What about my uncle?" Jenny demanded, fear already in her voice.

Christy hated being the one to tell her, and outside in front of everyone wasn't a good place either. "It's so loud out here. Let's go inside where we can talk." Christy led the way inside, beginning to worry that she was handling this all wrong.

"Christy, what is this all about?" Jenny was beginning to have tears forming in her eyes. "You're scaring me."

"Sorry, Jenny. I'm handling this all wrong. Come on. Let's go to Mrs. Smith's office where we can talk." Christy put her arm around her shoulder to lead her toward Mrs. Smith's office.

"He's dead, isn't he?" Pain was evident in her voice.

Christy was glad the door to the counselor's office was just a short distance down the hall. She opened the door and led Jenny inside. "I'm so sorry, Jenny. I shouldn't have said anything outside like I did."

"Tell me!" Jenny was really upset by now. "Please tell me the truth."

"Your uncle Ben was killed in Afghanistan. It was on the news this morning."

"No!" Jenny cried. "Please no!" She was crying in earnest now, and all Christy could do was put her arms around her and hold her while she cried. She couldn't help but think that this could be her one day. There was always that chance.

Mrs. Smith walked up and moved them on into the office and closed the door. She directed them over to a sofa that took up one wall.

"Her uncle was killed in Afghanistan. She didn't know."

"I'm so sorry, Jenny." Mrs. Smith said. "Would you like me to call your dad?"

Jenny just sat there so small and sad. "I don't think he knows, and I don't know how to tell him." The anguish in her voice made Christy cry.

Mrs. Smith passed both girls tissues. "It will be okay, Jenny. I'll call someone to go let him know."

Christy could hear Mrs. Smith speaking to the principal, and then she made another call a short time later. It was hard to tell how long they had been in her office before the phone rang. Mrs. Smith answered it and talked with someone else.

"Is there a chance that this is just a terrible mistake?" Jenny asked, hope evident in her voice.

"I only wish I could say it was so," Mrs. Smith crossed the room to where Jenny sat.

"It is all so unfair. Uncle Ben is such a wonderful person. He can't be gone."

"I know he was," Mrs. Smith agreed.

"Do Aunt Julia and Sarah know?" Jenny asked.

"If it was on the news this morning, they should have been informed earlier," Christy told her.

"Dad doesn't watch the news anymore and seldom answers the phone. So even if someone tried to get him word, he probably wouldn't answer the phone. Sometimes he doesn't answer the door when people come over. He's been like that since he came home from Iraq. He has what they call PTSD; I guess you know that stands for post-traumatic stress disorder."

"I'm sorry to hear that, Jenny," Mrs. Smith replied. "Your dad went through a lot in Iraq."

"He's getting help, but he is so different than when he left. He never smiles anymore, and he sits and stares into space a lot of the time. He doesn't talk about it, but he often has really bad headaches. He will answer me when I talk to him, but he seldom starts a conversation."

"He will again. It just takes time. What about your mother?"

"Mom left before Dad was injured and was having problems. Of course that didn't help him much," Jenny responded bitterly. "I don't even know where she is."

Sitting beside her friend, Christy found herself wanting to cry again. None of them had any idea Jenny had been going through all of this with her parents as well as dealing with the death of a friend. She had been blamed for the accident that killed her friend and ended a Razorback's career the year before. Summer had been almost over before all the details had come to light and people found out what really happened that night.

The phone rang, and Mrs. Smith moved over to the

desk to answer it. After a few minutes, she said, "I will tell her."

Turning back around, she looked at both girls. "Bob Warren is going to tell your dad, Jenny. I just talked to him, and he said that Sharon, his wife, is on her way to pick you up and take you home. She will be here in a few minutes. Is there anything that you need before she gets here?"

Jenny shook her head and then looked at Christy. "Will you stay until she gets here?"

Christy looked at Mrs. Smith and saw her nod to say she would before saying, "Of course I will. I just wish there was something I could do." She took out a piece of paper from her notebook and wrote her cell phone number on it, along with her home number. She handed it to Jenny. "Call me if you need me, and it doesn't matter what time it is. I know this is hard, and I will be praying for you and your family. Sarah is going to need you. Just remember we will be thinking of you, and if there is anything you need, just let me know."

"Thanks, Christy. I will call if I need to talk."

The phone rang again, and Mrs. Smith answered it before writing Christy a note for being late for class. Leaving the office together, Christy went one way down the hall, and Mrs. Smith walked the other way with Jenny toward the office. Christy stopped by the restroom on her way to class. Her eyes were red from crying so she wet a paper towel, and she patted her eyes to see if she could repair any of the damage that her tears had caused before heading to class.

She paused for a moment and bowed her head. *Lord,*

*please be with Jenny and her family. They need Your comfort right now at this moment. I need You to please be with Dad and Sam and keep them safe. May they soon get to come home. In Jesus' Name I pray.*

A few minutes later, she entered her first-period class. Mr. Coleman was at the front of the room talking. After handing him the note, she took the first empty seat she came to at the front of the classroom. It was hard to focus. She badly wanted to escape the harsh reality of the last hour. She just sat there for a time listening to the teacher but not really listening either. All she could think about was it could have been her instead of Jenny sitting in Mrs. Smith's office being told her father or brother was dead. Statistically the odds were more in her favorite than Jenny because she had two family members in a war zone. Her question about Coach Johnson and why she wouldn't be coaching the girl basketball team seemed so irrelevant now. Her heart hurt so bad that all she wanted to do was cry. She was so absorbed in her thoughts that when Mr. Coleman asked her for a solution to a problem, she didn't even know what the problem was. At the last minute, the answer was whispered from behind.

Without giving it any thought, she repeated, "194,000 miles." Then she felt guilty for not knowing what the problem was and not working it herself.

"How many got that answer?" Mr. Coleman paused for a moment, giving everyone a chance to raise their hands. "That's exactly right. Is there anyone who needs this last problem worked out on the board?"

*Great now he will probably ask me to put it on the board, and I don't even know what it is.*

"No one?"

Christy sighed in relief.

"Okay, for our next class period, I want all of you to take a look at section 1.2 and 1.3 and answer the even problems two through twenty, in each section. Also take a look at this problem and see if you can develop a strategy to solve it." Mr. Coleman projected the problem onto the board for the class to copy. "You will have to set the problem up and show the steps or strategy that you used to arrive at your solution."

There were several groans as students started copying down the problem. Christy relaxed after being saved from not having to show how she got the answer and recorded the problem in her notebook. She promised herself she would focus more when in class from now on so this wouldn't happen again.

Someone at the back said, "This is only the first day in this class, and we already have homework?"

Mr. Coleman smiled. "We have a lot to cover, but we will start out slow and not overexert those brain cells too much the first few days. Just keep in mind that at the end of this course, that you will be taking a test so you can receive college credit for this class."

When the bell rang, Christy turned around to tell the student behind her thanks. He was the guy she had seen in church on Sunday morning, and he was so handsome it made her feel breathless. She completely forgot what she intended to say to him. He was tall, close to six feet, with blond hair and the bluest eyes. His hair style was long, but he wore it pulled back in a ponytail. He looked different from the other students, someone who definitely knew who he was and where he wanted to go.

She blushed because she knew she was staring at him but couldn't seem to help it. *What was wrong with her heart?* It was beating double time. She had never reacted like this around a guy before. Willing herself to stay focused and for her heart to beat normally, she continued to look into his eyes.

"Hi, I am Aaron Smith," he said with a grin on his face, as if he knew the effect he was having on her.

"Thanks," she finally got out, but for the life of her, she couldn't think of her name as she stood there with a silly smile on her face.

He shrugged his shoulders. "No problem." Before he was given a chance to say anything else, Bill Matthew slapped him on the shoulder.

"Come on, Aaron, I want to catch up with Liz and Sherri before our next class." Bill walked around Christy without acknowledging she was standing there.

Bill was a senior too, but he had little time for anyone outside his own group of friends.

"See you around," Aaron said as he turned to follow his friend from the classroom.

Christy finally managed to push the strange way the new student made her feel aside and gathered up her things to leave the classroom. She caught up with Anne and Karri in the hall as they changed classes. This time they were headed to AP English together.

"What was going on with Jenny?" Anne asked as they walked down the hall together.

"Her uncle died, and she didn't know. Mrs. Smith took care of getting her home," Christy replied, not wanting to think about the bad news that had taken over her day. "Tell me why Coach Johnson isn't coaching us this year." She didn't want to think about soldiers dying when her father or brother could be facing terrible danger at this very moment.

"They're adopting twin boys. The call came yesterday afternoon for them to come pick up their babies if they still wanted to adopt," Karri answered.

"That's wonderful for them," Christy replied. "I know they will be wonderful parents, and they have been trying to adopt for a while."

"When they went to pick up the babies, the neighborhood got together a surprise welcome-home party for them," Karri added. "I tried to call you, but you didn't answer. I don't think I have ever seen anyone so happy."

"We must have been outside and didn't hear the phone. I wish we could have come." Christy sighed. "I wonder who our coach will be now."

"Why would you worry about that Jesus Girl?" A voice behind her asked. "It's not like it will affect you."

She didn't have to turn around to know Liz was behind her. "Lucky for me, it's not your decision who gets to play or make the team," Christy answered, although she knew that statement might not be completely true the way Liz and her friends on the team had of freezing out other players in the past.

As she looked at the tall pretty blond, she couldn't help

but notice her expensive clothes and tall, slim figure. Liz always dressed well, wore the right makeup, and looked like she had just stepped off the page of a fashion magazine. Christy couldn't help feeling short and awkward whenever she was around her. Still, even with all she had going for her, she only envied Liz for her height. She had found out more than once how mean and spiteful she could be.

"Just thought I would warn you before you get your hopes up," Liz replied sweetly. "You'll be way out of your league again this year, just like the last two." The smile on her face gave a clue to the chance she thought Christy had of making the team. "Of course, you do make a good team manager."

Before Christy could think of anything to say, Mrs. Scott, the Spanish teacher, said, "Come on students. Get to class. The bell is about to ring."

"Can you believe her?" Anne asked as they took their seats just as the bell rang.

"Don't let her get to you," Karri whispered from the seat behind Christy. "You've got as good a chance of making the team this year as anyone."

"Hello! My name is Miss Marshall. Many of you know me already from last year's Enrichment Program. I am looking forward to a great year with all of you. Before we get started, there's paperwork for everyone to fill out before each of you get to tell me a little about yourself."

The class looked around at each other with expressions that said, "Oh no, not again." Christy saw Aaron enter the room and take a seat in the front near Liz. Until now the English class had been made up of the same students as it had been for the past two years with no new faces.

Sighing quietly, Christy relaxed in her seat and started to fill out the forms her teacher was passing out, waiting to hear more information about the new guy.

Finally, each student was given a chance to come to the front of the room to speak. When it came Aaron's turn, he said he had moved to Hamburg just this past summer with his father, stepmother, and two brothers. His father had been in the military until retiring recently. He was interested in writing and taking pictures and thought he would enjoy the class.

A few minutes later, Christy gave her name and told a little about herself. Once she was finished, she let her thoughts go back to Liz's comments in the hallway. Liz was wrong. She would play, and she couldn't wait to prove her wrong. Her mind kept returning to Jenny and how sad she had been as she left her earlier.

*Please, Lord, comfort Jenny and her family at this time and continue to watch over Dad and Sam.*

# 3

After lunch, the day seemed to drag, and Christy decided it was going to take forever for the bell to ring, signaling the last block of the day. Finally it did, and Christy, along with Anna, Karri, and Tonya headed for the dressing room. There was a lot of chatter and laughing going on as the girls got dressed out for the first practice of the season. Christy felt excited as well as a little scared as she headed out onto the court. The feel of the basketball as it slapped her hand as she dribbled felt so natural and right. She noticed that more girls than usual were trying out this year. Still, she felt she had a good chance of making the team as she dribbled to the top of key and fired a jump shot that sailed through the air, touching nothing but net.

"Nice shot, Christy!" Anna shouted. "Bet you can't do that twice!"

Christy had followed the ball to the hoop, getting her own rebound. Dribbling once more to the top of the key, she pulled up and shot another jump shot that sailed through the net with a soft swish.

"Oh my, you have been practicing," Karri exclaimed as she ran up beside Christy and gave her a high five. "Not bad. Not bad at all." There was a big smile on her face as her eyes met her friends. "I have a feeling thing are about to get interesting around here."

Christy felt good. Maybe this was an omen that she would do well this year. Girls on both ends of the court continued to shoot and rebound the ball until they heard the sound of a whistle, signaling an end to the warm-ups.

Coach Riley, a tall, thin man in his late twenties, was standing at one side of the court. "Come on over and take a seat," he said as he motioned toward the bleachers. He and his wife had joined the teaching staff at Hamburg High the year before. Sue Riley taught business classes, and he coached the boy's football and basketball teams. The players really liked him.

Everyone hurried to take a seat where they could hear what he had to say.

Once everyone was settled, he said, "I'm glad to see so many of you trying out for basketball this year. I know some of you from last year, but I see some new faces as well. I wish all of you good luck for this coming season. I know some of you are disappointed about Coach Johnson not being back, but it you could see how happy she and her husband are with their new family, you would be happy for them."

He paused for a moment before continuing; "Now it's time to get down to the business of what we are here for.

I am to practice with you until they find a replacement, so I hope you are ready for some hard work!"

True to his word, they began working on drills they were all familiar with. Most involved running. They ran forward and backward, and they shuffled sideways, changing directions each time the whistle sounded while in a guarding stance. They ran dribbling and passing drills. They practiced dribbling right- and left-handed, setting screens, and shooting layups and jump shots. Christy had worked on all of these drills the entire summer and felt energized as they continued to work out.

By the time Coach Riley called it a day, he had kept his word when he had promised them it would be hard work.

He again called them over to sit down, and he gave them a short moment to get settled before he said, "Today was the beginning. There are many more things we will need to work on while waiting to find out who will be your next coach. Now go home and rest because tomorrow will be even tougher."

Christy left practice that day feeling good. She couldn't help but notice while on the basketball court that she seemed to be one of the better shooters and ball handlers. Finally, after all the long hours she had put in during the summer was about to pay off.

*Thank you, Lord. I know without your help I could not do this. You said if I would believe, then all things are possible. Well, God, I do believe, and I will continue to work hard to show You how much I want to be a part of this team.*

The smell of fresh baked cookies was in the air, and there were two packages sitting on the kitchen table waiting to be sealed when Christy arrived home from school. Taking a glass from the cabinet and milk from the refrigerator, she poured herself a glass of milk. She moved over to a barstool and took a chocolate chip cookie from a cookie jar sitting on the cabinet.

"Mmm, this is just what I needed," she told her mother, who walked into the kitchen from the front of the house.

"Hey, I thought I heard you come in. Did you have a good day?"

"It didn't begin too well. Jenny was at school and hadn't heard about her uncle yet. I also found out that Coach Johnson isn't coaching us this year."

"Actually, I learned the same thing about lunch time today when Gran came by. We went to Harrison's and purchased a few things for their twins and took them by their house. They are beautiful little boys, and I don't think I have ever seen anyone happier than Coach Johnson and her husband."

"I'm really going to miss her not coaching, but I can be happy for her too. Those two little boys are really lucky to have her for a mother."

"She said to tell you to come by and see the boys anytime you want, and she will be calling on you to babysit sometime in the future,"

"Wow, twins?" Christy said. "I imagine they won't need me for a while."

"You're probably right." Her mother answered with a laugh. "They have a sub for her right now?"

"They don't, but Coach Riley is working with us until

they find someone. He really worked us hard today for our first practice. That's why I needed this snack so much, I need some extra energy." She raised her empty glass and smiled at her mother. "I see you are sending some cookies to Dad and Sam."

"I was going to ask you to run the packages to the post office. I thought you might have something you would want to put in before we seal them up."

"As a matter of fact, I have letters to include and a new disk for Sam that I got this past weekend. Give me a minute, and I will get them. We can get these sealed so I can get them in the mail today." Christy ran upstairs and got the items, reappearing a few minutes later handing them to her mother to place in the boxes.

"Did you hear anything else today about the soldiers who were killed?" Christy asked.

"You already know Ben Masters was from Hot Springs. He was married to Jenny's aunt. They have a seventeen-year-old daughter, Sarah and five-year-old twin boys. The other man, John Thomas, was from Mountain Home. He was the same age as Sam. They had their pictures on the noon news. I just feel so badly for these families and wish there was more that we could do."

"I know, but prayers are really all anyone can do right now." Then she asks the question that had been on her mind a lot that day. "Mom, have you thought about not watching and listening to so much news on the war?"

"Yes, I have, but I want to know what is going on. I keep finding myself in front of the television with CNN off and on all day or on the computer. It is like I can't help myself. Besides so many people in our country act so detached from what is going on. Part of it is because it has gone on for so long, September 11, 2001, seems like a distance memory, but one thing I can tell you is exactly what I was doing when the planes flew into the towers and when they fell.

Shortly after that, we were at war, and we should never forget any of the men and women who are servicing our country and are sacrificing so much. Their families are right there beside them each step of the way, and it is important that we remember that and not just because we are a part of that family, but because it is the right thing to do.  When there is something we can do here at home to help each other, we need to do it. You know not everyone can be a soldier like your Dad and Sam, but everyone can do something." Mary finished sealing the first package closed and began taping the second one.

"I just want Dad and Sam home safe," Christy said after a short pause. "I just wish people would remember that this is the land of the free because of the brave."

"Just remember God is in control and He knows what He is doing. I know it is hard sometimes to just turn it all over to Him, but that is what He tells us to do and trust Him to take care of our problems."

"I know. Sometimes it is really hard to do. Do you ever wonder what people who don't have a God like ours to turn their problems over to must feel like?"

"Sad and discouraged, I would imagine. That is why He wants us to share Him with others. Plant the seed, and He will take care of the rest."

"Mom, I love you, and I've said this before. Thank

you for raising me up in the knowledge of God." Christy walked over and gave her mother a hug for a long moment.

"Thank you for being the wonderful daughter you are and for not being afraid to speak the name of God and tell others about Jesus."

"You and Dad taught me all I know," she admitted as she smiled at her mother.

"Oh my, look at the time. You will have to hurry to get these to the post office and in the mail today."

"I'm on my way." Christy took the money her mother handed her and grabbed her purse from the counter. They both carried a package out to the jeep.

Ten minutes later, she was circling the block at the post office for a second time before finding a parking place in front. Normally there wasn't a problem in locating an empty parking space, but today everyone seemed to be at the post office. She quickly gathered up the packages and the mailing labels that packages being sent to the troops required. As she hurried up the steps, she was wondering how she was going to open the door without having to put something down.

Just before reaching the door, she heard someone call her name. "Christy, wait up!"

She recognized the voice as Aaron, the boy in her math and English classes. And when she glanced around, he was hurrying up the steps toward her.

He opened the door. "It is Christy?"

"Yes, and thanks." She was surprised to see him again so soon. She felt herself blushing and wondered if he knew that she thought he was attractive.

Moving ahead of him, she joined a line of people

waiting for service. "Are you mailing something too?" She asked just to have something to say as they waited in line.

He held out a yellow card. "I am working for the local newspaper after school." He grinned. "They sent me to pick up a package."

"Do you get to write articles?"

"Actually I get to write articles and take pictures. The job has helped me decide journalism could be a career where taking pictures has always been more of a hobby than anything else."

"Hello, Christy," the postmaster greeted as she stepped up to place her packages on the counter. "How's your dad and Sam?"

"We think they are fine. The unit they are with lost some men yesterday. We heard about it on the news this morning."

"I'm sorry to hear that," he replied as he weighted the boxes and punched in information on his computer. "You tell them that we are praying for them when you talked to them again."

"Thanks. I will let them know. I am sure they appreciate all the prayers they can get."

"That will be twenty-four dollars and fifty-five cents."

She passed him thirty dollars and waited for her change. Once she had her change and receipt, she went to walk away.

"Christy, could you wait for me?" Aaron requested.

She paused in surprise as she looked back. He gave the postmaster the yellow pickup slip. While the postmaster went to find the item, he smiled at her.

"This shouldn't take but a minute."

"I will wait for you by the door," she said as she moved further away from the counter as there were still several people standing in line behind Aaron. She couldn't help but wonder what he wanted to talk to her about.

A few moments later, he rounded the corner carrying a large package. This time she opened the door for him. He carried it out to his jeep and placed it in the back before turning around to talk.

"I'm glad I ran into you," he said as he walked back over to where she was parked. "I have seen you at church a couple of times. I want to tell you how much I liked the Fourth of July program on the square."

"Thanks. I felt honored to be able to perform as part of the program that night," she answered, flattered that he had even noticed her.

"My family has traveled all over with the military, but the program on the square was one of the best I've seen."

"It is the norm around here. Our citizens really care about the men and women serving our country."

"Couldn't help but notice you shared your belief in God when you performed. You even prayed with the crowd," Aaron said.

"Actually, I hadn't planned to say what I did and finish with a prayer. It just happened. I felt in my heart at that moment a pressing need to pray for our country, our soldiers, and their families.'

"Not everyone agrees with you about the God thing," he added.

"It's not my intentions to offend anyone when I talk about and pray to God."

"Just so you know, I'm not a believer." Aaron declared.

"You were at church, so I thought ..." she began.

"Only because my dad makes me go."

A sad look came over her face before she said, "I'm sorry."

"I just find it hard to believe in something or someone I cannot see. You talk about God like He is your best friend."

"I talk to God because He is my best friend," she stated.

"A lot of people talk about you being a little obsessed on topics concerning God."

"I guess you could say that about me." She smiles.

"Bill said the school allows you to meet each week with other students as part of the Christian fellowship at school."

"Yes, in fact we are having our first meeting for this school year tomorrow at seven thirty in Mrs. Craig's room. Anyone can come and can bring along a friend. We talk to each other about God and plan activities like See You at the Pole, which will be coming up at the end of September." Her heart gave an extra beat hoping Aaron might join them. "You are welcome to come join us."

"I think I will have to pass on that, and I'm pretty sure my friends aren't interested either. You've known Bill, Liz and Sherri a lot longer than I have. They make fun of you and your group of friends, which I am sure you already know."

"I do know what they say about us Christians," Christy paused. "But any student at Hamburg High is welcome to join us."

"Don't you care what they say about you?" He looked back at her waiting for her reaction to his question.

"I care more about what God thinks of me," she responded, still smiling. "God loves us, including you, Aaron, so much that he gave His Son Jesus to died on a cross for our sins."

"Don't you talk about anything else? You do know most students our age think about and talk about other things."

"Yeah, I know, and most of the time its garbage in, garbage out," she said.

"What do you mean by that?" He asked.

"Have you really listened to what most students around you are talking about? If not, I challenge you to listen to the negative comments, the way they disrespect some students, the bad language they use, and the bullying.

"I tune most of the negative stuff out. What if I wanted to go out on a date with you? I'm not going to want to talk about God at all."

"First of all, I am not going to change who I am so I can go on a date with you. Second, I have to wonder why you're so against hearing about God. Are you afraid I might convince you to give God a chance?"

"You're still going to tell me about God?" His somber expression told her he didn't like her answer.

"Yeah, every chance I get." Christy said watching him turn to leave.

"I've got to get back to work." Raising a hand, he waved before walking away.

"You're welcome to join us in the morning," she called

before he got in his jeep. He didn't react, so she doubted she would see him the next morning.

Christy drove home with concern in her heart about the conversation she had just had with Aaron. *Did he really want to go a date with me? Should she even consider going out with him, knowing how he felt about God.* The day had begun on a sad note, and the fact that Aaron was not open to learning more about God made her day even more disappointing.

*Thank You, Lord, for loving us. I pray for Aaron. I pray that he will at some point in the near future want to know You. Help me to know what to say to help him if I get the chance. Guide my steps, Lord, so I can stay on the path You have planned for me. Thank You for the blessing in my life. Amen.*

# 4

The number of students at the meeting the following morning was a nice surprise. Christy recognized many from the junior high campus that had been very active two years before when she was a freshman. She kept glancing around the room, looking at all the new faces, knowing it was Aaron's face she was hopeful of seeing. At almost the last moment, he slipped quietly into the room and took a seat near the back. She couldn't help feeling thrilled he had shown up but noticed he had a camera around his neck.

Jarred Scott smiled at the students in the room before starting the meeting. "Welcome to the first meeting of this new school year. We are proud that you want to be part of the Christian fellowship at Hamburg High. If you will bow your head we will open this year with a prayer of thanksgiving."

"Lord, we pray that You will help us to share Your Word with each other and help us to grow. Help us to live in such a way that others can see You in us and we can be examples for those who have not found You yet. Thank You for all who are here and lead and guide us in the way You want us to go this school year. Help us to learn from Your Word. Help us to stand up for You and be able to share our faith with others so they too can find out how much You love each of us. Amen."

There was a short silence before Karri began passing out information about some of their goals for the coming year. "Our first study starting next week begins in Psalms. Notice we have a short form to fill out, and you can mention things you would like to discuss in our weekly studies. A calendar will be filled out and shared at the next meeting. We will have some of the planned activities on it, plus a space to add as we decided on other things to talk and discuss. Next week we will begin to discuss our plans for See You at the Pole, which is scheduled for the last Wednesday in September. Now Jarred will lead us in a worship song."

Jarred had his guitar out and sat on a stool at the front of the room. He begins to strum the strings and play the tune to "What a Friend We Have in Jesus," and students started to join in singing the words. Some waited until the chorus while others just hummed along.

Christy was the next up. She held up three roses for all to see. "Aren't these beautiful," she commented before passing them to students. As the roses circulated around the room, she told students, "You can pluck a petal if you wish."

She didn't say anything for a couple minutes until the roses were brought back to the front of the room and she held them up for everyone to see. All three had only a few petals left on them.

"Are they as beautiful as before?"

"No," several students responded at the same time.

"Many of your lives start out like the beautiful roses once you have accepted the Lord as your Savior. Keep in mind the world will never leave us alone. Satan will always try and steal your influence and try to pull you away from the Lord. He can't take away your salvation once you accept Jesus as your Savior, but he will do everything he can to cause you to sin. And if you let him take away your walk and your witness for God, then you too shall be like the flowers, beautiful at first, but soon you can see not so attractive if you let sin eat away at you." She paused for a moment."

"You may wonder. What can I do when Satan is chasing me? When you're not sure what to do, your *Bible* is your guide on learning about God and what He expects you to do in your walk. I encourage each of you to spend time in His Word each day. Set aside time and spend it in study and prayer with Him. In Psalm 1:1-3 it says, "Blessed is the man that walks not in the counsel of the ungodly, nor stands in the way of sinners, nor sits in the seat of the scornful. But his delight is in the law of the Lord; and in his law doth he meditates day and night. And he shall be like a tree planted by the rivers of water, that brings forth his fruit in his season; his leaf also shall not wither; and whatsoever he does shall prosper."

Christy again paused for a moment to let what she said sink in. "How can we know what He wants for us? The answer can be found in His Word, the *Bible*. What if you are new to all of this and just want to know where to start reading in your *Bible*. I would recommend starting with the gospel of John. It is here that you can gain knowledge of who Jesus was, why He came, what He did so you can have eternal life. Please join me in studying God's Word while also helping more people come to know Him, for He has promised that He will prosper us. If there is anyone here that does not know God as their Savior, I hope you will take a look at the bookmark that we gave out this morning. It has the steps on it to help you accept Jesus as your Lord and Savior."

"For some of you who are struggling with temptations, the one thing that helps me stay on course when I am tempted is to say the name Jesus. It is hard to sin when you bring Jesus to mind, especially when you are reminded of what he went through to pay the price for our sins. Should anyone have any questions, please ask any of us, and we will do our best to answer them."

Jarred again took over. "Thank you, Christy, for the devotional today. We need each of you to finish filling out the tear-out section in your bulletin and leave it here in this basket on the desk. We would like you to spend the rest of our time introducing yourself to each other. Please join us in a closing prayer."

"Lord, we thank You for each person who attended today and had a part in the program. Give us the knowledge in what is right to believe and strength to do Your will. Help us to be a light in this community and help us to not stray from our aim of spreading Your Word. In Jesus Name we pray."

Christy glanced around the room and smiled as she

listened to the friendly conversations taking place between students. Several students stopped her to tell her they liked the devotional.

She worked her way across the room to where Aaron was talking to several students. "Hi," she said when he finished talking. "Glad you made it."

He held up his camera. "I am taking pictures for the yearbook," he stated with a smile that warmed his eyes.

"Hope you will come back," she responded, but before she could add anything else, there were several students that walked up and started talking to them.

Christy listen in for a few minutes before politely leaving them to move around the room. Again she spends most of her time just listening to the conversations in the room. Karri and Anna joined her near the front of the room a short time later.

"A great crowd for a first meeting," Anne replied. "Did you notice the new guy, Aaron, I think, joined us."

"I know. I invited him." Christy laughed when both girls looked at her in surprise.

"There are a lot more than were here last year," Karri said with a big grin on her face as she held up the information slips.

"I was hoping maybe Tonya and some of her friends would join us," Christy added. "It is almost time to go to class."

"Maybe they will come next week," Anne told her.

Jarred came to the front of the room to ask, "Karri have you counted them yet?"

"Just finished," Karri answered. "There were forty-two students here today."

"Good group for a first meeting." Jarred turned to leave the room that was becoming empty since it was almost time for the first bell.

Christy, Anna, and Karri were in the same American history class that was just a couple of doors down, so they didn't have to hurry to class since the bell had not rang. "I like B days because we get to start the day together," Anna said as they walked the short distance toward the first block classroom.

Mr. McCall was at the door as they approached. "Good morning, ladies. I hope you are happy about being here first block."

"You know we love America history so early in the morning." Karri laughed as she came through the door. "Do we have assigned seats?"

"No, I believe we will see how you do the first few class periods. If we have no problems, you can sit where you would like."

They choose the second seat in the three center rows of the room. Christy took the center seat with Anne on her right and Karri on her left. The bell rang, and the room was soon full of students. The seats toward the back filled up first, and when Liz, Sherri, and Aaron arrived they had to take the last empty seats left, which were in the front center of the room. Aaron followed the two girls so he took the seat in front of Karri because Liz had taken the one in front of Anne and Sherri was seated in front of Christy.

Mr. McCall had them fill out paperwork while he was busy taking roll. Once that was done, he said, "You will continue to sit where you are for a few days until I have everyone's name matched with your faces. Now, if you will, we are going to take a little quiz." He was smiling as several students murmured their dissatisfaction.

The quiz wasn't too bad. The questions were mostly about who the President of the United States was now, which two main parties were running candidates for president in the election, which candidate represented each party, and what kind of history was being made in this election.

Once the students had a chance to answer the questions, Mr. McCall used his computer and pulled up pictures and short video clips that helped answer the questions. The class had several chances to discuss some of the politics that had taken place as the races came down to each of the conventions and a presidential candidate and vice president running mates were named for each party.

He passed out an assignment sheet that would cover the next several weeks, which would include watching highlights of both conventions in class and what their assignments for each section would be. He encouraged them to take an interest in what was going on in America and develop a voice and learn to think for themselves.

They were to keep journals about what they were learning and to write opinions about what took place in the election. By the time the first semester was over, they would have a new president and vice president as well as a journal that was to be turned in on Friday after election night on Tuesday for a grade worth three hundred points. They were to write about their feelings and ideas as they discussed and watched history being made. A few years earlier, Hillary Rodham Clinton, had been the first female

Democratic nominee to ever run for President of the United States and Christy felt pride that it was possible for another woman to have this chance in the next election. Donald Trump, the Republican nominee in that election had won. Since then, Kamala Harris, had been elected as the first female vice president in the land.

The class would begin their study with how presidents were elected and how important electoral votes were for the election of a candidate. The first assignment was for each of them to write a short paper on their thoughts on the election. To note what made each candidate stand out and what qualities made them right for the position they were running for. Mr. McCall had made the class so interesting that the class period went by quickly. It was hard to believe it was time to change classes.

Christy, Anne, and Karri separated for their next class but joined back up for lunch and then Mrs. Craig's Chemistry class. The day went by quickly, and in no time, Christy found herself back on the basketball court, practicing for a place on the team. Coach Riley kept his word about how tough the practice would be and worked them extremely hard. He believed in hard work and no shortcuts at each practice. The practice followed most of the routine of the day before. The last twenty minutes, he had them line up at both ends of the court around the free throw line and shoot three times and then rotate.

Liz and Christy lined up at the same goal. Both made their first three shots with both getting encouragements from their friends. The second time the same thing happened.

"You're just being lucky," Liz said to Christy in a low tone so no one else could hear.

"Perhaps." Christy responded with a big smile on her face, just enjoying the moment.

The third time, they lined up side-by-side. One would shoot then the other. Liz went first, and Christy was answering each shot by making hers. The frustration was beginning to show on Liz's face, and she missed her last shot.

Before Christy could shoot, Coach Riley blew his whistle and called all of them over to have a short pep talk before dismissing them.

"Okay girls," Coach Riley began. "One of the number-one things all of you need to work on is free throws. I see some of you have already been doing that. Liz, Christy, Tonya, and Sherri, that was quite impressive just now. The second thing I want you to keep in mind is that there is nothing that will replace teamwork. You play as a team. You will win as a team. Now go home and get ready for another grueling practice tomorrow because I promise you the same and a little more."

Liz ignored Christy as they walked toward the dressing room. She wasn't happy about the missed shot, but she seemed to know that this was not the time or place to say anything. Karri and Anne slapped Christy on the back and gave her thumb ups.

Later while shooting basketball in her driveway, some of the day's stress disappeared. There was little time for much more than homework assignments and shooting her hundred free throws each day after school. Christy had just finished her last free throw when her cell phone rang. The number wasn't one she recognized as she pressed the button to talk.

"Hello." Christy said.

"Are you busy?" She recognized the voice on the other end of the line belonging to Jenny Reynolds.

"Jenny, it is good to hear from you, and of course I can talk. How are you doing?"

"Things are as well as can be expected. We have been in Hot Springs since Tuesday. The funeral is scheduled for Saturday, and I have a tremendous favor to ask."

"Sure."

"Well, I'm not sure you can do anything, but I'm not even sure how to ask."

"Jenny, you know I will help if I can."

"I know you will understand because of your dad and brother. Dad is not doing well with all of this. I'm really worried about him. Today we found out that those people who have been going around protesting at military funerals are coming here to protest on Saturday."

"Oh, Jenny I am sorry to hear that."

"I'm scarred Christy."

"Jenny, they can protest, but they can't get near you," Christy reassured her.

"No, it isn't me I'm afraid for. It's my dad. Christy, he has said something that makes me afraid if they show up, that he might do something terrible to them."

"You mean harm them?"

"That is putting it mildly. Seriously Christy, I don't want to lose my dad again. He has been doing better with his PTSD until all of this. We have got to prevent him from doing something stupid. I just don't know what or how. I can't talk to anyone here because it is just too hard on my aunt and Sarah."

"Would you like me to try and talk to Bob Warren? I know they are good friends, and he might have an idea of what he could do to help or arrange it so he could be there on Saturday."

"That might be a good idea. I will try and call again tomorrow. That doesn't give you much time to think of something, but we don't have a lot of time."

"I will see what I can come up with, and I will continue praying for you and your family," Christy replied before pushing the off button.

*"Lord, I really don't know what to do to help Jenny. Would you please help her dad to be okay. Those people who plan to protest Lord, could you persuade them not to go to Hot Springs on Saturday. I know you are wiser than I could ever be and can take care of this problem. Just help me, Lord, know what You want me to do. Amen."*

It was later that evening after she and her mother talked to Bob Warren that Christy got an idea that might work. She was looking at the signs the group used as they protested. They were always so negative and filled with hatred and had such a bad overtone. Perhaps they needed to see some that were directed back at them with a message of love instead of hate. After all, Jesus said, "Do unto others as you would have them do unto you." And to "Love one another."

Taking out her notebook, she began writing down messages she would like to share with this group, messages that would tell them they should do good, not evil. As she wrote and made notes, a peace came over her that helped her know this could be a good thing and would please the Lord.

# 5

On Friday of their second week with Coach Riley, he called them over for his daily pep talk at the end of practice. "Girls, today was our last practice together because Monday your new coach will be here. I really see a lot of promise here, and I hope you will continue to work hard for Coach Thomas when she takes over. I look forward to seeing you play, and I hope you'll remember teamwork is the ingredient that plays an important part in any team's ability to be winners. Work together, and you will do just fine."

"Do you know anything about her?" Liz asked.

"I only know her name is Coach Thomas. I was only informed myself just before practice today. All of you will get to meet her on Monday."

Christy was leaving practice with mixed feelings. She would miss Coach Riley. He had worked them hard, and he had given her words of encouragement several times. "You may be small, but you play with more hearts than I have seen in a player in a long time. You're a good outside shooter, and that will bring your guard out. You have the speed to get free for a layup, and if you're picked up, you can dish the ball off to your open man."

"Coach Riley, I want to thank you for all the help and advice you have given me."

"Christy, it has been truly a pleasure coaching you. The biggest pleasure for me is the tremendous difference one summer has made in your playing," he told her.

"There were lots of areas for improvement from last year?" Christy said, knowing she was being truthful.

"I wouldn't exactly say you were bad. Last year you were not the mature player that you have become over the summer. You have developed into quite a shooter, but I think the main difference is that you are playing with so much confidence. In past years, I think you used your lack of height as the reason for not getting to play. I'm glad you didn't let that hinder you from discovering that it isn't just the height of a player the coach wants, but what is in here." He touched his chest where his heart was. "To play the game well, you have to love the game. From your hard work and dedication, I can tell that you do love the game."

"I just want to play for the Lady Lions," was all she could think to say.

"I really believe that I will see you out there this year. Good luck," Coach Riley declared with a big smile on his face as he turned and walked away.

Christy went to get changed with a good feeling about the coming basketball season. She had set the goal of making the team, but now she knew that making the team would only be a small part of what she aimed for. She would set a goal. Not only would she be on this year's team, but she would also be more than a benchwarmer. Monday seemed a long way away when you couldn't wait to meet your new coach and get down to the business of working for a starting position.

*Thank you, Lord, for helping me work hard to obtain my dream. I know from Your Word that if I have faith as a mustard seed, nothing will be impossible for You to help me accomplish. Please let all the hard work be enough to help me make the team this year. I hope You will be with all of us as we try and work out an answer for Jenny and her dad. I Love You, Lord.*

The scene in Christy's living room a few hours later was chaotic as a group of her friends joined her in trying to come up with more ideas for signs for the funeral the next day. The low murmuring provided a chance for her to catch her breath and wonder for the hundredth time if what they were about to share the next day was the right thing to do. She was out of ideas and out of time. She had worked since Wednesday night on the signs that they now had finished. She was hopeful that her friends could add some more to those that were ready to go. Perhaps someone would have a better idea. *Please, Lord, guide us with some good ideas.*

"Christy, these really look good. I don't believe they will go unnoticed, and I pray they will impact those who read them." Anne said as she held one up for everyone to see.

"As most of you are aware, Jenny's uncle's funeral is tomorrow. She called me Wednesday and told me that the people that are going around the country protesting military funerals are planning to protest tomorrow and that she is worried about it. I am asking all of you to try and come up with some signs that will fit in with the theme of those I have been working on. Bob Warren has promised that he will be with Jenny's family all day tomorrow and we are not to worry about anything. He is the one that is picking up these signs later tonight so they will be ready for the teams of students from Sarah's school and others who plan to line the route around the church tomorrow." Christy paused for a moment to see if anyone wanted to say anything.

"I've seen the protesters' display signs, but I have never seen any like these. They really do have a good message on them," Jarred stated as he walked around observing the messages on the signs Christy had already finished.

"I would never have thought to use signs as a defense to the protesters."

"I'm still not sure this is the Christian thing to do," Betty Smith said. "We don't want to do something that could make matters worse."

"Maybe we could find out where they are and let the air out of their tires so they would be late getting there," one student suggested. "I know Arkansas now has a law that they cannot protest thirty minutes before a funeral and can't be within a hundred feet of where the service is taking place."

"We don't want to do anything that would get us in trouble," someone else added. "My parents would really be upset with me if I got caught doing something illegal."

"We aren't going to flatten anyone's tires. What I was thinking is that I know all of you have seen some of the terrible signs that they display. As you see these signs have a message of hope. Perhaps we could come up with some others that would send a message back to them. You may think I am crazy, but I have given this a lot of thought. I got the idea that these people call themselves warning the American people we are a sinful nation and God is punished us. Where it is true that God does hate the sin, I think they are wrong in the hate messages they preach about God hates gays and our soldiers."

"I thought perhaps we could display some of our own signs that would send a message to the protesters in a similar way and remind them they are off course in what they are saying and doing. Where God does hate the sin, it isn't the sinner he hates, but the sin itself."

"Then I thought about it being important that we find ways to reach people about the gospel of Jesus Christ and how these people have turned so many people off by the way they are preaching their message. They portray our Lord as someone who is killing our soldiers and punishing our nation. They portray Him as someone who hates instead of loves. We have the right to counter some of their signs with those of our own. One of the messages I think is important for them to see and know is in this world that is full of turmoil and suffering, we are told to pray for one another and do what we can to alleviate suffering. Everything I know about God is the opposite of what they are preaching."

"They already have their minds set so. What could we say that would make a difference to them?" Betty questioned, looking as though she thought the idea wouldn't work.

"Oh, I thought perhaps they need to be reminded God loves them in spite of the sins they are committing. We are praying for our nation, and they could join us. That we are praying for them. I hope you can help me come up with some better ones."

"Jenny told me Sarah's friends are taking care of lining the road early just because of the protestors' plans. The veterans and bikers are also planning to get there early. Bob Warren told me he had contacted a couple of people he knew, and they will be there trying to spare the family from seeing or hearing any of this group's drama. He is coming by later this evening to pick up our signs so they can be in place early tomorrow morning."

"So where is our sign-making material?" Karri asked.

"I, for one, don't like these people and think they should just stay home if they can't respect the dead," Jared added.

"What if we divide into groups and come up with ideas of what we want to put on a sign?" Betty asked.

"That sounds like a good idea. Each group can brainstorm, and we will write ideas down and decide what we want on our signs," Anne told them while Christy took poster paper and scroll paper sticks out. The paint was already out on the table.

"Christy, I just can't believe some of these signs that

you have already made," Alice said while looking at the signs. "It is not like you to do something like this. You are the one that always does what is right."

"I happen to believe what these signs say is what this group needs to hear. We can be a bigger impact together if we stand together. Our military men and women are important to me and to this country, and if they die defending it, their families shouldn't be punished twice because the law can't stop these people from shouting their hatred at them. It is important that we not let their signs go unanswered. Perhaps they won't listen, but maybe others will see and hear our message over theirs."

Jared stood up and asked, "Is there anyone who doesn't want to participate?" He waited a full minute. "If no one wants out, then let us take some time to draw up plans and decide what we make into a sign. Let's get our strategies going. Christy, since you have us working on this plan, how about ordering us some pizzas? I'm starved."

"You're always starving." Everyone laughed and shook their heads in agreement. Christy made a face and added, "I am ahead of you and already ordered pizzas."

The doorbell rang, and Christy went to answer, thinking it was the pizza being delivered. Aaron and his brother, Bobby, were standing there. Bobby, a tenth grader, had his guitar across his shoulder. He was there to be a part of the group's worship team later that evening.

"Hey, Bobby, glad you could make it," Christy said as she saw who was there. "Come on in and make yourself at home."

"What time do you need me to come back and pick Bobby up?" Aaron asked.

"Would you like to stay too?" Christy asked as she saw the pizza delivery pulling up. "Pizza has arrived, and there is plenty."

"Stay, Aaron. You might enjoy it," Bobby told him as Christy paid for the pizza and gave the driver a tip.

"You sure?" Aaron asked as he took some of the pizzas from Christy.

"Come on. Everyone is starving, and you can help me set up the food so they can eat."

Going back inside, Christy couldn't help but be thrilled that Aaron had decided to stay. She wasn't sure how he would like their worship time later in the evening, but for now he was going to eat with them. They took the pizzas into the kitchen and placed them on the cabinet. They could hear students laughing and talking in the other rooms.

"Sounds like you have a large group here," Aaron said as he helps put ice in the glasses Christy set out as they were getting ready for the others to come and get their food.

Christy got out paper plates and napkins before rounding up a box of plastic spoons and forks. The last thing was the cake her mother had made for refreshments and the batch of cookies that she had cooked herself when she got home from school.

"You think we are ready?" Aaron only shook his head for yes. "Then let's help our plates before we get stampeded, which is what will happen as soon as we say food is ready."

"Whatever you say." Aaron grabbed a plate and got two pieces of pizza and cheese breadsticks with ranch dipping sauce. He fixed a glass of Coke.

As soon as Christy had her plate made, she moved over to the living room door and told everyone dinner was ready. Taking her plate and glass of tea, she and Aaron moved out of the way and went out on the patio to eat. It was a lot quieter outside, and a light breeze kept the temperature pleasant.

"Is it always like this?"

"Not always, but when we get together, we do have a lot of people who come and join in. You see, I'm not the religious enthusiast all by myself. I do have backup."

"You are not at all what I thought," Aaron stated.

"To be fair, most of the time most people aren't. It is like we stereotype people and don't give them a chance to know who the real person is."

Other students came out and joined them. Jarred pulled up a chair next to Christy and looked over at Aaron. "Glad you are joining us."

"Thanks,"

"He came with me," Bobby said as he sat at the next table over.

"Hey, Bobby," Jarred said. "You been practicing that new song that I gave you?"

"Sure have, and I am ready to play whenever you are."

"Great. We will set up soon and see what you can do," Jarred told him before looking back at Aaron. "You play or sing?"

"He can, but you won't get him to play," Bobby said before Aaron could say anything.

"I play a little guitar, but I'm fine watching others play." Aaron gave Bobby one of those looks that said, "Wait till we get away from here."

"If you ever want to join in, you are more than welcome to try out. Just let me know," Jarred added. "We're always looking for new talent."

"Thanks, but I believe I'll just watch," Aaron said.

Several of the girls were asking Christy where something was, and she had to get up and leave the group. She took her empty plate to the trash can that had been set up early before everyone got there and headed inside. She looked over the new signs and gave her approval before moving them over to join the other ones that Bob Warren would be coming to pick up.

Karri and Anne joined her in the kitchen and helped her with the cleanup while others were visiting different areas of the house. Looking up, she saw Aaron with Jarred, who was setting up the music instruments for their practice. She couldn't help but wonder if he would enjoy their practice or have something to go back and tell his friends. *Oh well. Time would tell.*

"Hey, Christy," Jarred called. "You about ready?"

"Yes," she replied as she went over and took a seat at the piano. "Let's open with a word of prayer. Jarred, would you pray for us?"

"Dear Lord, we come tonight to thank You for the many ways You have blessed us and our friends. We ask You to be with the families who lost their loved ones fighting for our country and comfort them. We ask, Lord, that the signs we made be used in a way that will help comfort the Masters' family and speak to the group that protests at soldier's funerals. May they realize that they should be showing a loving message instead of one of hate. Lord, we want to now praise your Holy Name and give honor to You."

Christy started playing the music to "Nothing But the Blood." Jarred started the words with the first verse, and then the group joined in with, "Oh precious is the flow... that makes me white as snow... No other fount I know ... Nothing but the blood... Nothing but the blood of Jesus..." They went on to a song they had used for praise during the Bible school they had helped with during the summer vacation.

Alice asked, "Can we do the other one too? You know the one that says, "There your mercy and grace was free... There your pardon multiplied to me... There my burdened sold found liberty... At Calvary."

Christy started playing the music, and they all joined in to sing it.

"What about Blessed Redeemer?" Karri said when they finished.

Again Christy started to play, but this time she sang, "Up Calvary's mountain one dreadful morn...Walked Christ my Savior weary and worn... Facing for sinners death on the cross... That He might save them from endless loss..."

The group joined in on the chorus, "Blessed Redeemer... Precious Redeemer... Seems now I see Him on Calvary's tree... Wounded and bleeding for sinners pleading... Blind and unheeding... Dying for me..."

Then she changed over to "Tis so sweet to trust in Jesus... Just to take Him at His word... Just to rest upon His promise... Just to know "Thus saith the Lord"... Jesus, Jesus, how I trust Him... How I've proved Him o'er and o'er… Jesus, Jesus, precious Jesus… O for grace to trust Him more…"

Christy looked over at Aaron several times during their worship time and noticed he was listening and joining in with singing when they did a repeat choir when he knew the words. They played and sang for close to an hour before Jarred and Bobby played and sang the new song they had been working on together.

"Christy, do you have a song you want to share?" Jarred asked.

"I'm saving mine for Sunday morning service," she replied.

"Anyone else?" When no one else spoke up, Jarred said, "Then let's dismiss with a prayer. Thank You, Lord, for this time of worship and for each person here, and we pray for Your strength and comfort for those who are hurting and need Your grace, Lord. We pray for the family of Ben Masters and for those who will be there tomorrow at his funeral. We ask for Your guidance and protection over our men and women who are serving our country. We also ask for guidance and wisdom for those who are making decisions that lead our country that they will be wise in their endeavors. We pray for a lost world that they will come to know You before it is too late. Amen."

Again Aaron helped take the music instruments down and pack up. Christy was busy helping everyone get signs to the front door when the doorbell rang. This time it was Bob Warren there to get the signs. Everyone helped get them out to his SUV, where he placed them in a safe place in the back so they wouldn't get messed up.

"Thank you for all your work on these signs. I can

see a lot of thought went into them," Bob said as the last sign was placed on top of the others.

"I just hope those who need to see them will." Christy replied. "Thank you for all you are doing to help Jenny feel better about her dad."

"Glad you called and ask for my help."

When she turned around to go back inside, she noticed Aaron was standing to the side with Bobby, who had his guitar.

"Glad you decided to join us tonight," Christy told them. "Bobby, your song with Jarred was amazing."

"Thanks," Bobby was glowing. "I haven't had this much fun in a long time."

"Thanks for letting me stay." Aaron said.

Christy could not tell if Aaron felt as Bobby did, but as least he had stayed until the end. "You are welcome anytime." She smiled at him, and this time he grinned back.

"We had better go." Aaron said as they walked toward his jeep.

It was only later that she had a few minutes to think about the night's events and felt again a need to pray.

*Lord, thank You so much for everyone who had a part in the signs we made. Please let this work not do or say anything that will harm Your message. In my heart, I feel this is right and good. If You have another way, Lord, don't let us get in Your way. I pray especially for Aaron that he will become open to learning more about You and will want to one day know You as his Lord and Savior. In Your Name I pray.*

# 6

It was a warm Saturday afternoon with a soft breeze moving the flag that draped the coffin of Major Ben Masters. Christy stood with several of her classmates under an old oak tree off to the side of the tent where the family sat. She was near enough to see the tears that were running down the faces of both Jenny and Sarah as they held each other's hand in the front row. Next to Sarah sat her two younger twin brothers, both too young to really comprehend what was going on. Her heart ached for her friends, but she knew there was little she could do about it. The sound of the twenty-one guns salute rang out over the peaceful cemetery setting seemed out of place before the sound of "Taps" drifted out over the large crowd.

Moments later soldiers were folding the flag and handing it to the major's widow, a small token of the sacrifice that her husband had made for his country. The preacher led a final prayer, and it was over. People started moving around, but Christy and her friends stayed still.

They did not want to intrude on the family's last moments at the end. Jenny looked up and saw them, and she said something to Sarah beside her. Soon other people were between them, and Christy could no longer see her.

"Do we want to try and make it back to the jeep?" Anne asked.

"Christy!" Jenny had made her way over to their sides. "Thanks for coming today and all you did."

"How is your dad?"

"Good," she replied. "Did the people show up?"

"I don't know, but if they did, they found a scene of signs all up and down the streets with messages of God's Words," Anne said a smile on her face. "We heard there was an accident on the highway, and the protestors were stuck in traffic and didn't get here in time to set up. There were so many people here there wasn't anywhere near the church they could have gotten anyway."

"I am thankful," Jenny looked back toward her family. "Dad is looking for me so I've got to go, but thanks for coming, and I will see all of you next week at school."

"We will be praying for all of you," Christy said, giving Jenny another hug.

As they walked back to where they had been able to park the jeep, they meet up with several of the other students. Christy didn't know about the rest of them, but she was so relieved that there wasn't a face-off with the protestors. She didn't know if the protestors saw the messages on their signs, but she did know that a TV crew had filmed the signs so perhaps they would get the messages. The one that she was proud to claim was the one that said, "Life After Death!" Ben Master To Die Is Gain! He Knew Who His Savior Was. "Do You?""

"We are parked about a block further down than you. Give us a few minutes to make it to our cars, and you can let us out," Jarred said as he approached.

Falling into step, they continued on in a comfortable silence. "I guess our prayers were answered today," he added as they reached the jeep.

"I believe they were," Christy replied, feeling at peace. A smile tugged at her lips. "Just shows you that God is in control here, not us."

"Text us when you reach your car, and we will pull out. I think it might take a while for traffic to clear out."

Karri and Anne both joined Christy in her jeep. Several other students from Hamburg waved as they passed by where they sat.

"I had no idea there would be so many people here for the funeral," Karri said as they watched people leaving.

Christy frowned when she looked up and saw Liz, Sherri, Bill, and Aaron walking by. She was wishing she didn't feel so jealous all of a sudden. Catching herself biting her lip, she was glad to hear her cell phone beep so they could go.

Looking down at her screen, she saw the text "ready to go," and she responded with "ok" before starting her engine and pulling out into the traffic. She let Jarred and Betty out when she got to where they were trying to get out on the road.

They stopped in Monticello to have something to eat. Christy realized she hadn't eaten all day when they ordered. She had been too nervous to eat breakfast, knowing what they were doing that day. Now she realized she was depending on her own strength when she left home that morning, not expecting to be let out of the plans that they had intended to carry out. For the first time, she realized she had prayed for a way out but had not expected an answer so promptly.

*Forgive me, Lord for not having more faith that You would take care of any problem.*

She checked her iPhone and noticed she had a text message from her mother telling her that she and her grandmother were going back by the Masters' home before they left Hot Springs. They would not be late, but she could have Karri and Anne stay overnight if she wanted. After texting her mother back to let her know she had received the message, she texted that she would let her know when she reached home.

Looking up, she saw and heard Liz and Sherri coming through the door. They were both laughing about something, and just behind them was Betty Smith. The look that was on Betty's face was one of concern when she looked over at Christy. *Was that a guilty look on her face? I must be mistaken. Why would Betty feel guilty about anything?*

Liz tossed her long blonde hair over her shoulder and walked quickly over to the counter to place her order. Sherri was one step behind her still laughing at whatever was so funny. Bill and Aaron came in a moment later, but Christy looked away before she could make eye contact with Aaron, pretending not to see him. Why did it upset her that Aaron seems to be with Sherri?

Christy took a bite of her taco, but it didn't taste

as good as it had a few minutes earlier. Looking over at Karri and Anne, she noticed that they both were enjoying their food.

"Would you two like to spend the night at my house?" she asked.

"Well, yeah, but I'll have to check with my mom first," Karri responded.

"I will have to check with my parents when I get home, but sure I can," Anne added.

"Hey, Christy," Aaron's voice had Christy turning around as their group took the table beside theirs.

Christy gave him a brief smile and said, "Hi."

"That was the first military funeral I have ever been to. I have seen them on TV, but it isn't the same, is it?" Aaron placed the tray with his food on the table. "All the signs that lined the streets, I didn't expect anything like that. Got several pictures on my cell phone."

"Pretty amazing if you ask me," Christy replied.

Christy's iPhone started to vibrate, and she used the diversion to ignore Liz and Sherri as they took up seats facing her. She didn't recognize the number, but she pushed the button to accept the call.

A moment later she heard the voice of her brother at the other end saying, "Hey, sis!"

"Sam! Is that you?" Christy exclaimed. "It is so good to hear your voice." She pushed back from the table and motioned to the others she was going outside to take the call. Tossing her dark hair over her shoulder, she walked quickly outside.

"Just having a little downtime and wanting to hear

from home," Sam replied. "Miss all of you a lot. I am looking forward to being able to come home soon."

"We know. We miss you too," Christy responded, knowing the tears that she had held back all day were about to flow. She moved over to the jeep and sat in the driver's seat while they talked.

"What's going on there?" he asked.

"I'm on my way home from Major Masters' funeral. Karri, Anne, and I stopped in Monticello for something to eat."

"Let me guess, Taco Bell."

Christy laughed. "You know me too well."

"How was the funeral? We had our own memorial for the major here a couple of days ago. All of our men are down over his death. He was a good man. One of a kind. He showed daily that he believed in God and let all of us know it too."

"I know. How is Dad?"

"He is taking the major's death pretty hard. Now he has more responsibility, and I don't get to see as much of him as I did."

"I just wish you were both home," Christy said with a crack in her voice. "Have you heard anything about when you might get to come home?"

"Nothing," he answered. "The latest situation here has made a difference in our activities and may indicate something. I just don't know."

"Did you receive my last package?"

"Yeah, it was waiting for me when we returned to the barracks. Thanks for the music and batteries. Especially all the mail from back home it means a lot."

"Be sure to tell Dad that we miss him and love him when you see him."

"I will. How is basketball going this year?"

"Really well. I hope you get home in time to see me play."

"You're that good?" Sam asked. "I told you, didn't I."

"You did, and I listened to some of your advice. You just hurry home so you get to see me play."

"I will," Sam responded. "Listen, I hate to get off, but I have to go. Tell Mom I will call her tonight if I can."

"I will, and you take care of yourself. And Sam."

"Yeah?"

"I love you."

"I know you do and ditto that from me. You take care of yourself."

Then the line went dead. Christy couldn't control the tears that were flowing down her face. Putting her head down on the steering wheel, she cried for several minutes before she got control of her tears.

*Please, Lord, be with my brother and Dad and bring them home safely. Please lead and guide them in making the right decisions concerning their safety. Lord, please guide our leaders so they can bring our men and women home soon.*

"Christy, are you okay?" Aaron asked as he approached the jeep.

"I will be." She smiled at him through her tears. "When my brother and dad are no longer in harm's way."

"I'm sorry; I know it is hard to be away from them for so long." Aaron said. She could tell by the way he looked and how he said it that he knew exactly what she was feeling.

"I guess you had plenty of practice with deployments too."

"Not just deployments. My mom moved away from where my dad was stationed after the divorce. I didn't get to see too much of my dad growing up." The look on his face was one of sadness too.

"I'm sorry Aaron," Christy told him.

"But before they could say anything else, Karri and Anne were getting in the jeep. Sherri walked up and put her arms around Aaron while Liz and Bill were walking over to get in Aaron's jeep.

"Don't be. There is nothing that will ever change that. Drive carefully."

"Come on, Aaron. We are ready to get home," Sherri said.

He walked away before she could say anything else.

Anne placed Christy's drink in the drink holder between the front seats. "I thought you might want your drink. We tossed the rest."

"How is Sam?" Karri asked.

"Okay. Ready to come home. Just wish this war would get over and there would be no need for military funerals or protests." She turned the key in the ignition to start the jeep.

Letting the other two talk, she forced thoughts of her family from her mind and drove home.

*Lord, You are able to do all things, and I thank You for being with us and with Jenny's family today. Please continue to watch over my dad and Sam. May they soon get to come home. Help me to be faithful to You because my life is so blessed because of You. I love You. Amen*

# 7

As luck would have it, Christy was the last player on the court for basketball practice on Monday. She had received a note to report to the office at the end of third block. When she arrived in the office, no one knew anything about the note, nor who had sent it. By the time she had gotten to the dressing room, everyone was on the court, and the sounds coming from the gym indicated practice was in progress. She heard the whistle blow. The new coach was issuing commands as she hurried onto the court.

"Glad you decided to join us, Rivers!" a voice boomed.

Christy turned toward the new coach. She was never given the chance to explain her tardiness because she noticed immediately the direct gaze and unyielding expression on the new coach's face."

"I expect you to be on time for practice. You owe me ten laps through the bleachers." With those few words said she had turned away and continued where she had left off with the other players. *Whew,* Christy thought, *what a way to start the first day with the new coach.*

She quickly ran the ten laps, thankful that she had worked so hard all summer.  As she ran, she couldn't help but notice Liz and her little group with their heads together whispering and giggling as she ran by them. She had just finished the last lap when Coach Thomas blew the whistle and motioned the girls to arrange themselves in a circle on the floor.

"Looks like you're getting off to a great start with the new coach," Liz whispered sarcastically as she moved by Christy on her way to sit beside her friends.

Christy didn't miss the gleeful gleam in Liz's blue eyes as she spoke to her or the giggles from her friends.

The snickers were quickly cut short when Coach Thomas began speaking. "I can tell you have been working hard the first couple of weeks, but I'm warning you now you're going to work even harder. Basketball is a very competitive game. You have to be in great shape to win, and we are going to win. If you aren't willing to be at practice on time and give practice your all, then you need to get your schedule changed." She looked straight at Christy when she said the last part.

The players were listening attentively to their new coach. She was down on one knee, her elbow resting on the other knee. Christy couldn't help but admire her. She was tall and slender with short blond hair that made her look like a young boy. There had been a lot of information passed around over the weekend about the new coach. She had received her bachelor's degree at the University of Arkansas at Fayetteville, where she had played for the

Lady Razorbacks. Later she received a master's from the University of Texas at Austin, where she had worked as an assistant coach for ten years. Christy couldn't help but wonder why anyone would give up a job like that to coach at a small high school in southeast Arkansas.

"If you work hard, we have a good chance of an outstanding season. Remember, your attitude has a lot to do with your game. We are going to work on aggressive man-on-man defensive, and this should help make our offense better. Now let's see what you can do."

They ran line drills before working on fundamentals. After the line drills, they begin with simple drills as simple as handling the basketball, dribbling, and passing. They worked on their guarding stance and movement. They moved on to working on pivots and fakes.

"Don't fake with just the ball," she told them. "Use everything. You want your opponent to think you're going to do one thing when you intend to do something else. You have to use the ball, along with your eyes, hands, and shoulders." She took the ball and showed them what she wanted before having them line up at the end of the court in several rows to practice faking and driving one-on-one.

Christy threw herself into the practice with all her energy. This was one of the things she liked, the thump of a basketball, the feeling of hard leather on her palms. After faking and driving around her guard, Christy changed places with Tonya and got into her guarding stance. She did a good job guarding Tonya as she tried to fake Christy out.

After finishing her turn and waiting another, she observed Coach Thomas showing Liz how to bend her knees more in her guarding stance and how to keep her eyes centered on her opponent and move with her. Coach Thomas definitely knew what she was doing.

By the end of practice that first day when a halt was called, there was not a player who didn't know what was in store for the days ahead. As Christy changed her clothes in the locker room, she tried not to think of the bad start she had gotten off to with the new coach. All around her, there was laughter and lighthearted conversations going on, but this only seemed to weigh heavier on Christy's troubled thoughts. She hadn't spoken one word to the new coach. Nor had the coach spoken directly to her after issuing the command for the ten laps unless you would call the suggestion to quit if you weren't willing to be on time. Talking about a start, she had really gotten off to a great one.

"Christy, why were you so late for practice?" Karri commented.

"I'll tell you about it later," Christy answered as her thoughts returned to the unsolved note.

*Where had it come from?* Christy hated unsolved mysteries. She looked around the dressing room for Liz but noticed she wasn't there.

"Why don't we meet at Sawyers for ice cream in about half an hour? Karri asked.

"Sounds great to me," Anne replied. "That will give me time to run by the library before I meet you there. I still need one more source for my English paper tomorrow."

"Okay with me," Christy said as they left the locker room.

The question of where Liz had got off to was answered

as soon as they left the locker room. Liz was standing outside the coach's office door, deep in conversation with Coach Thomas. Karri and Anne walked by them on their way out of the building as they left the gym by the exit that led out to the school parking lot where their rides would be.

Christy went back through the school building for her books. As she reached the door to the science room, she wondered if Mrs. Craig was still in her room since the door was open.

When she glanced in, Mrs. Craig was sitting behind her desk writing.

"Mrs. Craig, may I speak to you a moment?"

"Come in Christy. How can I help you?"

"I just wanted to ask you about the note for me to report to the office at the end of third block," Christy said as she approached Mrs. Craig's desk.

"Was there a problem?"

"I just wanted to know where it came from. When I got to the office no one seen to know anything about it."

"How strange," Mrs. Craig answered. "It was on the door when I came back from lunch today. I thought the office must have sent it, although they usually call over the intercom for things like that."

"That's all I needed. Thanks, Mrs. Craig."

"I hope you didn't have any problems because of the note," Mrs. Craig said as Christy was leaving. "I can give you a note if that would help."

"I was just curious as to where it came from," Christy said again.

There was little use in telling Mrs. Craig what

had happened. She couldn't undo the laps, or the first impression Coach Thomas had gotten of her.

"If I learn anything, I'll be sure to let you know," Mrs. Craig said.

She almost told Mrs. Craig not to worry about it. She was pretty sure who was behind the note. When she reached her jeep, there in bright-red letters was a note taped to the steering wheel that said, "DELAY TACTICS WORK WONDERS" with a big smiley face. Whether Liz was responsible for the note or not didn't matter because being delayed for practice had certainly worked at causing problems with Coach Thomas.

*Please forgive me, Lord, I am sure Liz is behind this, but I have no way of knowing for sure. Help me not to say something to her that I will later regret. Please lead and guide me in what I should do. Thank You, Lord, I Love You.*

When Christy arrived at Sawyers, Karri and Anne were already seated at a table upstairs on the balcony. The view was a good one of the downtown square of Hamburg. She had always liked sitting on the balcony and watching people come and go. It took only a few minutes to order and receive a vanilla milkshake before she was able to go upstairs and join her friends.

"Now just what happened to you today to make you so late for basketball practice?" Karri demanded as Christy slid into one of the chairs.

"Mrs. Craig gave me a note to report to the office after

third block," Christy replied. "When I got to the office, no one knew anything about it. Of course, by the time I got dressed out and to practice, I was late and had to run laps. I went back by and talked to Mrs. Craig before leaving school. She said the note was on the door when she got back from lunch." Last, she pulls out her phone and shows them a picture of the note left in her jeep.

"Liz is definitely behind this!" Karri exclaimed a little too loudly.

Christy looked around to make sure no one else was listening in on their conversation. There were a group of junior high girls seated near them, but they were sipping their sodas and listening to each other talk about boys. No one seemed interested in what was being said at the next table.

"More than likely, but not very provable," Christy responded in a low tone.

"Creative?" Karri said with a raised eyebrow at them.

"I don't understand that girl," Anne said. "She has everything going for her, yet she can't stand it if she isn't the center of attention."

"But I'm not in competition with her," Christy replied. "Why does she want to cause trouble for me?"

Karri and Anne looked at each other. "She doesn't even realize …" Karri stated.

"I know," Anne agreed.

"Come on, you two. If you know something that I don't, how about sharing."

"You're really good at basketball this year," Karri stated.

"That's a tremendous relief." Christy laughed.

"Especially since I have spent my entire summer working to make improvements."

"Well, you really have some moves that make people stop and watch you play," continued Anne. "What's more, Liz has been watching, a little nervously, I would say."

Christy continued to look confused. "I know I'm playing well. I can keep up with everyone, but I still don't see why this should upset Liz. She's still the best player we have."

"She sees you as a threat to her control of what she wants going on with the team. And she doesn't like the idea of sharing the limelight with you," Anne replied seriously.

"Me a threat?" Christy questioned. "You've really got to be imagining things."

"We aren't." Karri assured her.

"Look, we really don't know Liz put the note on the door," Christy said. "It could have been anyone."

"Oh, we know Liz didn't put it there," stated Anne. "She would be afraid of getting caught, but you know she knows who did."

"The question is, what are we going to do about it?" asked Karri.

"For now, I'm going to forget it," Christy responded.

"You're kidding!" Karri exclaimed. "You're going to let her get away with it."

"Just turn the other cheek?" Anne replied.

"Yes, you could say that. I'm serious about not causing problems for the team. You know as well as I do that if I said something without proof that Liz would have me for lunch. And no doubt, so would our new coach."

"Liz is not going to stop with just a note," Karri declared.

"Karri, we really don't know for sure that it was Liz. It could just as easily been someone else playing a joke at my expense," Christy responded.

"It was Liz. I can't prove it, but I know she's behind it," Karri stated. "This is just like last year."

"Last year I couldn't shoot." Christy said. "I know now that I didn't even deserve to play on last year's team."

"But Christy ..."

"No, Karri! I wasn't that good of a player. I knew it, and so did everyone else. There were others who deserved to be on the team more than I did." Christy replied.

"This year is different," Anne added.

"Yes, this year is going to be different. Liz or no one else is going to stop me from playing," Christy responded in a determined voice.

"Just watch your back," Karri replied. "I don't think this is over."

"Christy is right about causing problems for the team. There are those on the team who already follow Liz because she has been the leader for so long," Anne said. "If we say anything to Liz about this, it will just cause a bigger split."

"We're not saying anything. I think the least said is the better. You know, keep them guessing and not let them know they got to me."

"In other words, it never took place?" Anne answered.

"Exactly! I'm not interested in being the leader or anything else. I just want the chance to play. Can we change the subject?" Christy sighed. "We are beginning to sound like a broken record. What did you think about Coach Thomas?"

"I think she is going to be good for the team," Karri said.

"I believe she will be fair," Christy said cheerfully.

"Even after running laps?" Anne questioned.

"Sure, she has to be firm the first day," Christy conceded. "I think I admire her for that."

"I've got to go," Anne announced, looking at her watch. "It's almost five, and I still have to finish writing my paper for tomorrow."

"Me too," Christy added. "I promised Mom I would be home by five."

"I've got to finish my paper too," Karri stated as she looked at Christy. "How is yours coming?"

"I wrote mine this past weekend," Christy answered. "All I have to do is proofread it before uploading it."

"I wish that was all I had to do," Karri said. "I can't seem to get everything done. I still have math homework to do too."

"Do you need a ride home?" Christy asked when they reached the jeep.

"I think I will walk, it's just a couple of blocks from here." Karri replied as she turned and walked the other way.

"Good luck on the papers," Christy called. "What about you Anne?"

"Jeff is waiting on me at the library."

The fall afternoon was perfect for a ride with the top off in the jeep as her hair blew in the breeze. She spent the few minutes driving home, thinking about the events of the afternoon. One of the first things her mother was sure to ask about was what she thought of the new coach. One thing for sure, she wouldn't mention the bad start she had got off to. She wished her grandmother were home because she could sure use one of her positive pep talks.

Christy smiled as she could hear her now with one of her favorite sayings that was sure to boast ones spirit. The one that came to mind was, *"Just look at it this way. Things can't stay bad forever. They will either get worse, or they will get better. But one thing for sure, they won't stay the same."*

"Let's hope things get better, Gran," Christy said aloud. "Because I don't think they could get any worst, or at least I hope not."

*Please, Lord, help me to do what I need to do to get back on the right side of the coach. Let her give me a fair chance. Thank You for loving me. I love You.*

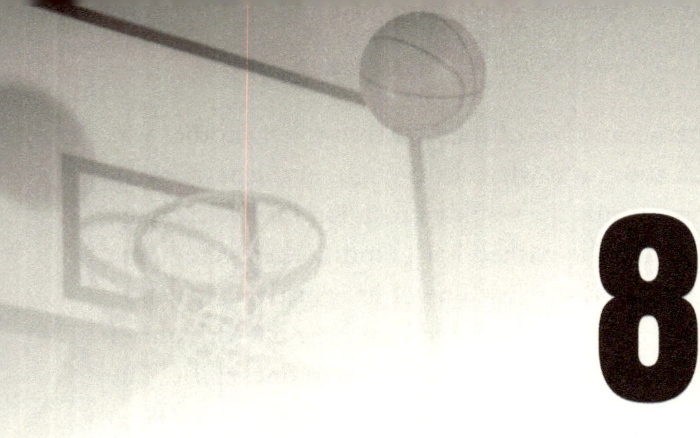

# 8

The next week went by without any more incidents like the first day. Christy wasn't late again for practice. Nor did she give Coach Thomas reason to be unhappy with her during practice. By the second week with Coach Thomas the players had settled into a pattern of warming up with a few minutes of shooting, then line drills, followed by dribbling and passing.

The players soon realized their Coach was a perfectionist. She expected nothing but the best from each player. She was very demanding and would have players repeat drills over and over until she was satisfied with their performance. All the girls were improving, and it was obvious Liz was in top form; in fact, she had never played as well. Coach Thomas had been working with her on developing a quick release on her inside shots that was paying off.

Liz had just faked her guard out and had sunk a basket that gently touched the backboard before dropping through the net. One of the players complimented her as she went to the end of the line, "That was awesome, Liz!"

"I know," Liz said triumphantly, never one for being modest. "But I should be getting good with all the extra practice I'm putting in."

"When do you find time for extra practice?" inquired Karri curiously.

"I'm coming before school twice a week, and staying after school two other days," Liz answered casually. "Coach Thomas has been helping me put in extra practice time since she knows how important it is to the team for me to get my shooting down right."

"Let's go, Rivers," the coach said, bouncing the ball to Christy who had been listening to Liz's explanations and hadn't noticed it was her turn. "I want you to fake, drive to the basket, and try a jump shot from corner post."

Christy took the ball and faked out her guard by faking to the right and going to the left. She stopped at the corner of the free-throw line, leaped, and shot. And swish! The arching shot dropped through the net. She was unaware that there was a gracefulness to the fluid movements that contributed to the overall effect. Christy knew the ball was going in as soon as it left her hand. She felt a surge of satisfaction knowing that she had done a good job.

"Not bad," commented the coach when Christy had finished.

Then she showed Samika Davidson, the guard, what she should do to better stay with the person she is guarding. She had Christy do it again while she demonstrated what she wanted. This time Christy was unable to get a shot off.

Coach Thomas's whistle brought all the players to a halt. "Now we will set up and run a few plays. Let me see Parker at center. Davidson and Jackson, you play the forward positions, and Arnold and Rivers, you're the guards. Arnold, you bring the ball down the floor and call the plays."

"Cook, Tucker, Wilson, Miller, and Taylor set up in defense positions. The rest of you pay attention. It will be your turn next. First, set up and bring the ball down the court on the three main plays we have been working on. The defense either needs to get the rebound or steal the ball and take it to the center court."

Sherri began a circular move with passes and breaks that hopefully would set up either Liz for an inside shot under the goal, or one of the forwards for an outside shot. Every time Sherri got a chance, she forced a pass into Liz. Already twice the guards had stolen the ball. Each time Coach Thomas blew the whistle and started the play again. The third time it happened, the whistle creased play once more.

"Not like that," scolded the coach, taking the ball from Tonya. "You've got to be patient and move the ball more. You can't tell the guards where you're going with the ball before you do it. Now let's try it again."

No one said a word. This time they moved the ball more, but it was obvious Sherry would rather get in trouble for throwing the ball to Liz than to pass it to Christy. Once she had thrown the ball up for a shot when she didn't have one to keep from passing the ball back to her.

Christy mainly passed the ball, and a couple of times, she was able to fake her guard out and drive on her. Both times when Liz's guard picked her up, she was able to dish the ball off to Liz, who put the ball up and in.

The second time it happened, the whistle sounded again.

Coach Thomas took the ball. "Did you see how Rivers did that, Arnold? I want to see more plays like that. When the guards are able to drive, you will be able to do one or two things. You will be able to shoot, or the guard will move over to pick you up, and then look for the player who will be open."

Coach Thomas paused a moment to see if she was understood. "Rivers, set it up and try screening for Davidson after passing off," she said as she gave the ball to Christy.

She started the play off by faking out her guard before making a pass to Simika, and then she set a screen for her. Simika dribbled once passed the ball back to Christy as she rolled toward the goal. Christy bounced pass the ball to Liz as Liz's guard picked her up under the goal. Once again Liz was able to put the ball up and through the hoop with the quick release shot she had been working on.

"Good play!" Coach Thomas shouted. "Try it again!"

This time Simika was able to take a set shot. The ball struck the far side of the rim and then bounced off toward the opposite side of the floor. A scramble was made for the ball with Karri coming up with it. She dribbled to the center court before giving the ball to Christy to set up and start the play again.

The next time, the play progressed as it had the first time, but when Liz's guard didn't move over to help out, Christy was able to pull up and shoot a short jump shot.

Coach Thomas blew the whistle once more to explain how the guards must work together to stop this type of play. Again, she demonstrated the guarding stance she wanted and expected to see.

"All right, Arnold, I want you to pass off and set a screen for Jackson."

They continued working on screening the rest of the practice. The whistle continued to blow each time something went wrong. Coach Thomas was very patient, but she would have them do a play over and over until they got it right. By the time practice was finished for the day, they were all physically weary and glad to head for the locker room.

As they changed clothes, everyone seemed to be laughing and talking about what they were doing for the weekend. Sherri and a couple of the other girls were talking about a party that Liz was throwing that night. It was the first Friday night without a football game since school had started.

"Are you coming, Karri?" Sherri asked. "I hear Barry Allison is going to be there. He was asking Liz this morning if you were coming."

"It does sound like fun," Karri said.

"I really hope all of you will try and come," Liz said as she walked over to where Karri, Anne, and Christy were. Tell Jeff and Ricky they are invited too,"

"Thanks, Liz," Karri answered. "I have to check with my mom first."

"Yeah, me too," Anne added.

"What about you, Christy?" Liz asked.

"If Karri and Anne go, I will," Christy answered.

"Great," Liz responded. "I look forward to seeing all of you later."

Once they were outside the locker room, Anne turned to Karri and demanded, "What do you mean you have to ask your mom?"

"Oh, Anne, wouldn't it be fun to go to the party. A lot of students are going."

"Are you crazy? This is one of Liz's parties," Anne responded.

"You will have to admit Liz has been nicer to all of us lately. Maybe she is ready to forget our past differences and try and be friends." Karri pleaded.

"That's what I'm worried about. Liz doesn't do nice and she has been too nice lately," Anne replied. "That's why I say she is up to something."

"Really, couldn't we go?" Karri pleaded again. "We don't have to stay a long time."

"I suppose it might be fun. What do you say, Christy? Want to go to one of Liz's famous parties?" Anne asked.

"Since we're spending the night with Karri tonight, I'd say she gets to decide on the entertainment," Christy replied.

"Let's go check with our parents," Anne said.

"We need to hurry. I still have to find something to wear." Karri headed for the door. "How do you think I should fix my hair?"

Christy and Anne just looked at each other and rolled their eyes. Little did they know that they would regret their decision before the night was over.

*Please, Lord, don't let this be a mistake. Maybe Liz is finally going to accept me on the team and we can be friends again. She has been really nice lately and I know what You say about forgiving others that have hurt us. I do forgive her, Lord, and I thank You for forgiving me and loving me in spite of my sins. Amen.*

# 9

The party was to begin at Liz's house around seven o'clock. Christy and Anne were beginning to think they were going to be late. Karri had changed clothes three times and fixed her hair four different ways before finally deciding to leave it down. Anne's brother, Jeff, had agreed to go and drive them as long as his friend, Ricky Davis, could come too. Karri assured him Liz had invited them both.

When they arrived, there were kids everywhere. Some were dancing to the loud music coming from a CD player; others were standing around talking. A few were fixing something to eat from a table filled with food.

"Glad you decided to come," Liz shouted over the loud music as they walked up to where she stood with several of her friends.

"Thanks for the invitation," Karri shouted back.

"Just join the fun. If you want something to eat help

yourself," Liz gazed past them like she was looking for someone else.

"Later we are going to do some fun games and go out to Bill's family's deer camp," Liz informed them. "I hope you will be able to go with us because that is where we will have some real fun. Make yourself at home and have a good time." She turned and walked away, followed close behind by Sherri.

Karri, Anne, and Christy walked over to the table to fix themselves a plate after Liz left them. Jeff and Ricky had already found the food. The noise coming from the CD player was so loud Christy wondered if the neighbors might complain.

After fixing a plate, she fixed a cup with ice from an ice chest and poured herself a glass of Coke. Several picnic tables sat up around the lawn. They moved over to where Jeff and Ricky were already seated beside some of their friends. They had chosen the table as far away from the CD speakers as possible.

Several people were dancing close by, but at least it was quiet enough they could talk. They hadn't been seated long before Sherri came by with a box of envelopes.

"You have to choose one of these to see what your group has to do before you can join us at the deer camp," she stated.

"What is it, like a scavenger hunt?" Jeff asked.

"Not exactly. It's more like a challenge that you have to accomplish," Sherri informed them. "Nothing too awful."

"Can we open it now, or do we wait until everyone else opens theirs? Anne asked.

"Oh, you can open it now," Sherri replied. "We want

to know if you accept the challenge before you leave the party." She laughed.

Christy had a funny feeling about the envelope as soon as she saw Karri choose one and opened it. Inside was a card with a short message.

Karri read it aloud. "You must visit the location of the mysterious light. Just follow the map on the back of the card. Once you reach the location marked X on the map, you must turn off the engine, turn out all lights, and wait at least fifteen minutes. If you have not seen the light in the time allotted, then you may leave. Of course, if you do see it, don't let it catch you."

"The light?" Anne said. "I've heard about it, but I thought it was just a tale kids told to scare people."

"There have been a lot of stories told about it," Jeff said. "I've been on a hayride out that way, but we didn't see any lights."

"What are some of the stories?" asked Karri.

"One story tells how a train ran over a man on the train tracks. The light is supposedly his ghost holding a lantern and looking for his head," Jeff explained.

"I've heard it comes up behind you and chases you. The next thing you know, it is in front of you," Ricky added. "Of course, I've never seen it, so I don't know if any of these tales are true.

"Are you saying this place is haunted or something?" Anne asked.

"No, I don't think so," answered Jeff. "I think it is something like the northern lights. People just add on tall tales to make it sound scarier."

"I hate to disappoint you, but I've even heard some

of the adults in my family talk about the light. I think there really is something. No one knows what it is for sure," Karri replied.

"I've heard a lot of people say they've seen the light," Jeff returned. "But I don't know if they were speaking the truth. You know how some people exaggerate things sometimes."

"Don't we all. But my question is why a ghost would need a light," Christy said.

"Don't ask me. I'm not saying it's true. I'm just telling you what I've heard," Jeff answered.

"What do you want to do?" Anne asked. "Do we go out there or not?"

"I think it would be fun!" Ricky added.

"Where have we heard those words before?" Anna asked Christy. They both laughed.

"Sounds like you're not too afraid to visit the light," Liz laughed as she walked up to where they were talking.

"Should we be?" Christy asked.

"I've been out there," Liz replied. "I didn't find it too frightening. Of course, some people scare easier than others."

"Did you see the light?" Anne asked.

"I'll tell you when we meet up at the camp." Liz voice became low. "That is if you don't chicken out. Or if the light doesn't get you first." With that theatrical challenge, she laughed and walked away.

"Don't worry, girls. We'll protect you," Jeff said.

"Yeah, Jeff and I will keep you out of harm's way." Ricky backed Jeff up.

"Is that supposed to make us feel better?" Christy asked.

Everyone laughed again. They finished eating and spent the next hour talking and laughing with other friends that had come to the party. Barry finally came over and asked Karri to dance. Ricky and Anne joined them leaving Jeff and Christy standing alone.

"Don't look now, but Alice Martin is looking over this way. I think she is jealous," Christy told Jeff.

"Really?" Jeff grinned. Everyone knew he and Alice liked each other, but they both were too shy to actually talk.

"Why don't you ask her to dance?" Christy asked.

"She'd probably say no," Jeff answered, looking a little nervous.

"You never know unless you ask. She might even say yes," Christy said encouraging her friend.

"You think she might?" He glanced over his shoulder.

"Go on. If you're going to brave the light, surely you can practice getting up your courage by asking a girl to dance."

Those last words must have convinced him because he finally walked over to talk to her. A few moments later, they were dancing and smiling at each other.

"Matchmaking, are we?"  A voice said from behind her that she recognized as Aaron Smith.

"Hi, Aaron," Christy smiled at him. "I didn't see you."

"I just arrived," Aaron said. "Enjoying the party?"

"I guess," Christy answered.

Even though she hadn't seen too much of Aaron lately outside of class, she thought he was one of the coolest guys she had ever met. He was certainly the first guy that she had ever felt something more than friendship toward.

"I guess you stay pretty busy with your part-time job with the paper?" Christy asked.

"I certainly have to plan my free time well. That's for sure. But I really like my job. I'm learning a lot about journalism."

"Do you want to dance?" he asked when a slow song started to play.

"Sure." she answered.

He took her hand and led her into the middle of the other couples. Christy put her hands around Aaron's neck as he put his hands around her waist.

It felt every bit as good as she had known it would to be held in his arms. She smiled and rested her head against his heart as they moved slowly back and forth, swaying to the music. Her heartbeat quickened when she tilted her head back and stared up at him because his heart wasn't beating normally either.

He looked into her eyes, and for a moment, Christy got the crazy idea he wanted to kiss her. She felt her cheeks going red and was glad the light was dim and no one could see. It was heavenly dancing with him, but all too soon the music came to an end. He led her toward the outside of the group of dancers and continued to hold onto her hand as they moved toward the food tables.

The magic ended when Liz's voice interrupted them. "Aaron, when did you arrive?" She tossed her long blond hair out of her face. A not-too-happy Sherri stood beside her.

"Liz," Aaron said. "I just arrived a few minutes ago."

"I didn't see you," Sherri exclaimed. "You've just got to dance with me before we leave."

"I believe Karri and Anne were looking for you," Liz told Christy a look in her eyes that said she was very angry about something.

Christy had already figured out she wasn't too pleased to find her dancing with Aaron. To make matters worse, at that moment Christy noticed Aaron was still holding her hand.

Aaron let go of Christy's hand. "Come on Sherri, let's dance."

Christy watched Aaron lead Sherri over to the dance area. She couldn't help but be glad that a fast song was playing. There was a smile on her face as she went to join her friends.

"Whoa!" Liz snapped, grabbing Christy's arm to keep her from walking away. "Sherri likes Aaron."

"So, what's wrong with that?" Christy asked.

"Nothing is wrong with that." Liz's blue eyes shooting daggers at her. "I would hate to see you get hurt."

"Aaron is a friend. That isn't going to change no matter who likes him."

"They are dating, and you don't have what it takes to steal Aaron from Sherri," Liz declared. "Leave him alone."

Christy's mouth dropped open. "Look, Aaron asks me to dance, not the other way around."

"Aaron was just being nice," Liz said quickly. "He likes Sherri. So remember you've been warned. If you get hurt, it is your own fault." Liz walked away.

Christy couldn't even begin to count the times that Liz had said those last words to her in the past two years.

Then she would walk away before she could ever think of something smart to say back to her. *Probably just as well,* Christy thought. *It's hard to argue with someone who always thinks they have the right answer to everything.*

"What was that all about?" Anne asked as she walked up.

"Just Liz being her usual self, I guess," Christy declared. "How much longer until we can go?"

"Soon I hope." Anne grinned. "Having fun yet?"

"Oh, can't you tell I'm having a blast? In fact, it wasn't too bad until Liz decided to boss me around," Christy said sarcastically.

"Well, at least you got to dance with Aaron," Anne replied. "You look cute together."

"Cute?" Christy smiled. "Well, the dance was worth having to put up with Liz."

*Thank You, Lord, for the friendship that I have with Aaron. Please don't let Liz spoil that too. I Love You.*

# 10

A short time later, the CD player was turned off.

"Hey, everyone!" Liz shouted. "We are ready to let you carry out your challenges before we meet up at the camp. Most of you already know where it is located, but if you don't, we have some maps for anyone who needs one. You've had a chance to look over your challenge. If you don't feel up to the challenge, let us know before you leave. Otherwise, let's get this show on the road!"

Cars were parked everywhere, so it took a few minutes for everyone to get in theirs and leave. Karri met them at the car. She told them she was riding with Barry and would see them at the deer camp. Christy and Anne got into the back seat of Jeff's four-doors Chevy while Ricky joined Jeff in the front with the map. Jeff pulled the car out onto the highway and turned south toward Crossett.

"You know where we're going?" Ricky asked.

"I studied the map before we left. I know the road

where we turn, so I'm pretty sure I can get us where we want to go," Jeff replied.

"Jeff, please put the radio on something decent to listen to!" Anne said.

Jeff turned the dial from station to station and finally settled on an oldies station.

"Wow, Liz sure puts on a party," Ricky declared. "I've never seen so much food at a party before."

Everyone laughed, knowing how well Ricky liked to eat.

"She certainly believes in organizing everything," Jeff responded. "Did you hear her order Aaron to dance with Sherri?"

"Yeah. I was standing right there," Christy said.

"I wish we could have just stayed there a couple of more hours," Anne added. "I really didn't want to go to the deer camp."

"Things will probably get pretty loud out there. I'll warn you now. There will be drinks out at the camp, something the Parker's wouldn't allow at their house," Ricky said. "Besides, the neighbors aren't likely to put up with the loud music into the night."

"I guess so, but I'm still surprised Liz's parents are letting the party go on so late."

"They may not know," Anne said.

"What do you mean? I thought they would be out at the camp too," Christy replied uneasily now. She knew her parents would not be too happy about a party with drinking and no adult supervision.

"Barry was telling us everyone will stay as late as they

wanted at the camp. No parents are going to be there," Ricky told them as if it was no big deal.

"I don't know about your parents, but mine aren't likely to be too pleased about that," Christy stated.

"Then simply don't tell them." Ricky told her.

"You mean lie?"

"No, simply don't mention it, if it doesn't come up." Ricky answered.

"How late are we going to stay?" Christy was getting nervous about the whole thing. She had never lied to her parents, not even by omitting something.

"Stop worrying. It won't be that late, and we aren't going to be drinking. You're with us, remember. Besides, you can always say we wouldn't leave." Jeff told her.

"I just think it's a mistake to go out there," Christy added, feeling more and more like they were making a bad decision.

Jeff turned off the highway onto a gravel road a short time later. He turned onto an old logging road. It was a little bumpy but wasn't too bad to drive down. As they drove deeper into the forest, they came to a Y where the road divided.

Jeff turned left. "Just a half mile now according to map," he said.

They finally came to a stop. Jeff turned off his motor and the car lights. It was really dark, and it took a few minutes for their eyes to adjust to the darkness around them. Gradually you could see the clearing the road made down through the dark shapes of the trees.

"Goodness, it's dark," Anne whispered like she was afraid to speak too loudly.

"I can't see anything," Ricky added. They heard nervousness in his voice.

"Maybe the light is just a tall tale," Jeff commented after several seconds.

"How much longer do we have to wait?" Anne whispered.

"We just got here." Jeff laughed.

"How will they know if we waited the full fifteen minutes?" Anne returned.

"You've got something there," Ricky agreed. "They aren't going to know if we stayed the full time. We can just take our time getting to the camp."

"I'm ready if you are." Jeff said.

"Look there in the opening behind us!" Anne cried. "What is that?"

An eerie white cloud drifted close to the ground in the distance behind them. A bright glow was coming from it.

"It looks like a light of some kind," Ricky muttered. "Do you think this is what they were talking about?"

"It's coming closer," Christy said in a frightened voice.

The light wavered and grew bigger and brighter. Christy's heartbeat grew louder. The mysterious glow floated up higher and was coming closer and closer.

"Do something, Jeff!" Anne shrieked.

Jeff had started the car and took off in the opposite direction of the light. They bumped over several holes in the road before he realized he didn't have his lights on. He turned his headlights on and barely missed a tree trunk by just inches. The road curved to the right as they continued bumping over more holes in the logging road.

Suddenly, as in slow motion, the road gave way. The car gave a hard jolt as it came to an unexpected stop.

Christy was thrown against her seat belt.

"What happened?" Ricky shouted.

"Why did we stop?" Anne added at almost the same time.

Jeff turned the motor off immediately and just sat there with the lights on. "Do you see anything?"

"No, but it was right behind us," Ricky said in a low voice.

"I don't see anything now!" Jeff stated as he looked around them.

"Why did we stop?" Anne asked again.

"I think we're stuck in the middle of a mudhole." Jeff murmured.

"Where did a mudhole come from?" Christy questioned. "It hasn't rained in weeks."

Jeff took a flashlight and directed its beams out the window onto the sluggish brown muck.

"Yeah, we're right in the middle of the largest mud hole I've ever seen," Jeff said dryly. "Wonder how it just happened to get here right in the middle of nowhere with no other signs of mud around."

"Oh no! we've been set up!" Christy declared.

"Some prank," Anne replied with a nervous giggle.

"I'm sorry if I don't find this very comical!" Jeff snapped.

"At least it explains the light. That seems to be gone now," Christy said relief in the voice.

"I've never been so scared in all my life!" Anne exclaimed.

"I think you're right. We've fallen hook, line, and sinker for someone's practical joke," Jeff agreed angrily. "Liz Parker had better hope my car isn't damaged."

"We are going to have to walk out of here," Ricky moaned. "This car isn't going anywhere."

"I'm afraid you're right." Jeff turned around in his seat and looked at Christy and Anne. "You two could stay with the car while Ricky and I go for help."

"Not going to happen! There is no way I am staying with the car!" Anne snapped. "Even if this is a setup, Christy and I are not staying here by ourselves."

"Take it easy Anne. You're going to need all your energy to walk out of here," Jeff replied. "You're right. Dad would have my hide if I left you two here alone."

"Don't try getting out just yet," Jeff told the girls before he pushed the car door open and stepped out into the slimy brown water. The mud quickly covered his shoes as they sank into the muddy depth, and he had a hard time moving toward the back of the car.

"Roll the back windows down," he said as he reached the back door of the car. "Ricky, you will have to try getting out on your side. We will piggyback the girls to dry ground. There is no need in them ruining their shoes and clothes."

"You could give me a ride on your back too," Ricky returned.

"Not likely," Jeff responded. "My shoes don't like this at all."

"What about my new cowboy boots?" Ricky complained. "My khakis! My Mom is going to have my hide for this!"

"I'm not carrying you!" Jeff laughed, showing the first sign of humor in the situation. "You can always pull your boots off."

"I think I'll take my chances with my mom murdering me," Ricky declared. "We have a long walk ahead of us."

"Okay, girls, you are going to have to climb out the windows," Jeff said.

Christy was sitting on Jeff's side of the car. She climbed out the window and took the flashlight to hold while he slowly carried her on his back through the sluggish goo. He almost slipped down. Only by catching onto the side of the car was he able to keep his balance. Finally he was able to set her down on dry ground.

"Good thing you girls don't weigh a ton," he said as he took the flashlight and directed the beam toward Ricky and Anne.

They had reached the back of the car, and Ricky was trying to keep his balance. Jeff stuck out his arm and helped him make it out of the mudhole without dropping Anne.

"Are y'all ready to walk out of here?" Jeff asked.

"Do we have to go back that way?" Anne asked. "I just know they are going to try and scare us again."

"We don't know where this road is going. It seems to go deeper into the woods," Jeff replied. "I'm afraid we are going to have to go back the way we came."

"What about the light?" Anne whispered.

"I thought you had decided it was staged for our benefit." Ricky answered.

"The way the light floated. How do you account for that?" Christy asked.

"Look, I don't know the answers, but I do know I don't plan on standing around here all night!" Jeff snapped. He started walking in the direction they had come. The others quickly followed him.

"I'm going to murder Liz," Anne grumbled.

They had been walking only a short time when Christy asked. "What time is it?"

"It's close to ten thirty," Jeff stated.

"It had been only half an hour since they had left Liz's house, but it seemed a lot longer. For a while they didn't talk at all. The silence in the woods was almost as eerie as the light had been earlier. Christy's heart sped up every time there was a slight sound or rustles in the underbrush. She couldn't shake the feeling of being watched. The air began to have a smoky haze the closer they got back to the road.

"Is it my imagination, or is it getting foggy?" Anne whispered.

"It is getting foggy," Jeff replied.

"Oh, great!" Anne declared. "Now all we need is to see that light again, and I think I'll expire right here on the spot."

"Why did you have to say that?" Ricky complained. "I don't even want to be reminded."

"We can hardly see where we're going," Christy whispered nervously. "Are you sure we aren't getting lost."

*Please keep us safe, Lord. Help us find our way out of here.*

"We're all right as long as we follow this road back to the main road," Jeff stated.

They had almost reached the Y when again they saw

a wispy glow. It started out as a small glow, but it grew bigger and bigger and brightened as it came toward them.

"Jeff!" Anne screamed as she and Christy grabbed each other. "What do we do?"

It was coming straight toward them. Christy hoped she was having a nightmare that she was about to wake up from. Jeff and Ricky grabbed the girls' hands and turned to run. This was no nightmare. They were all awake. The thought crossed Christy's mind that they were seeing the light but they might not get to tell the others about it.

*I'm sorry that I didn't listen to You, Lord. Please protect us.*

# 11

They had not taken more than a dozen steps when suddenly Jeff stopped and looked back.

"That's a truck!" Jeff said, relief evident in his voice. The sound of a vehicle was clearly audible as it came nearer.

"What if it's not Liz or some of the others? What if it's some of those drug people we are always hearing about?" Anne cried, fear evident in her voice.

"It's too late to worry about that," Jeff replied, moving to the side of the road as the vehicle came nearer.

The glare of the headlights blinded them as it pierced the fog for a moment until it pulled up even with them. They were then able to see it was a jeep.

For the second time that night, Christy was glad to hear Aaron's voice as he asked, "Need a lift?"

"How did you know we were here?" Jeff demanded, anger clearly in his voice.

"Karri was worried about you, so she had Barry find

out where you were." Aaron answered. "Barry refused to leave the party so Karri asked me if I would. Here I am."

"You weren't in on their plans?" Jeff asked again.

"I don't know what plans you're talking about," Aaron said. "Do you need a ride or not?"

"Sure and thanks." Jeff was calmer after deciding Aaron wasn't in on the prank that had been pulled on them.

Jeff pulled the front passenger's seat up and let the others climb into the back seat of the jeep. He then pushed it back into position and got in and fastened his seatbelt.

"We're sure glad you came to check on us," Ricky said from the back seat. "You saved us a lot of walking."

"What happened to your car?" Aaron asked.

"It's stuck in a big mudhole." Jeff replied.

"Are you joking?" Aaron asked with surprise in his voice.

"I wish I were," Jeff answered.

"Do you want to try and pull it out?"

"I don't think we should. It's stuck pretty badly. My dad would be pretty upset with me if I mess something up by trying to get it out. I'll get Dad to come help me with it in the daylight, and we can see what we are doing."

"Do you want to go home, or by the camp?" Aaron asked.

"Jeff, we really need to pick Karri up," Anne answered.

"I guess so," Jeff said grudgingly. "I'd rather go home."

"You're not going to start trouble if I take you out there, are you?" Aaron asked.

"Fighting isn't going to change anything. I'm already

planning to send Liz a bill for getting my car hauled out and cleaned up," Jeff replied.

"And for a new pair of cowboy boots," added Ricky. "My Mom is going to kill me when she sees these."

"Too bad we can't send her a bill for scaring us half to death," Anne whispered to Christy.

"Yeah, I know what you mean," Christy agreed. "I've never been so scared in all my life."

"Me either." Anne stated. "Just wait. Liz is going to pay for this. I don't know how yet, but she is."

The jeep sped through the trees, hitting holes and bouncing them around in the back. Aaron had been driving for several minutes before making a wide turn onto the gravel road, only slowing a little. Christy was glad to know they were out of the woods, and back on a well-traveled road. She also noticed the fog seemed to have disappeared. That was strange she had never noticed fog doing that before. One thing for sure, she didn't care to go searching for the light again. Once was enough. She shut her eyes and tried to relax.

It seemed no time at all before loud throbbing music greeted them when they arrived at the deer camp. To Christy, it seemed twice as loud as it had been back at Liz's house. Some boys were yelling and laughing over by a pickup truck. Liz, Sherri, and several others were standing around a log fire that had been built out in an open area. There were a lot of kids from school standing around that had not been at the party.  She even recognized two ninth grade girls. Karri stood beside Barry over by one of the pickups. She hurried over to the jeep when they came to a haul.

"It's about time you got here."

"What kept you?" Liz laughed behind her.

"You should know," Jeff replied.

Sherri greeted Aaron with a half-smile on her face as he got out of the jeep. "I thought you would never get back," she complained as she ran up to him and put her arms around his waist.

"How was the light?" Liz asked with a wicked sparker in her blue eyes. "What happened to your ride?"

"Cut it out Liz." Jeff said. "You already know."

"Know what?" Liz asked sweetly. "I don't know what you're talking about."

"Sure you do," Jeff returned. "But that's okay. I will send you a bill for the expenses of getting my car towed."

"Why would I pay your tow bill?" Liz giggled, covering her mouth with her hand.

"Because it is your fault that my car is stuck in a mudhole." Jeff glared.

"Surely, you didn't get stuck?" Liz sounded surprised.

If it hadn't been for the glee in her eyes, Christy might have believed she really didn't know anything about it.

"Look, I didn't tell you to go and drive off in some mudhole, and I certainly wasn't driving the car. You can't make me pay some bill that isn't my fault. Sorry."

"Karri, we're ready to go home," Christy added, feeling the tension mounting.

"You can't leave yet!" Sherri insisted. "Aaron just got back, and the fun is just starting. Come on. We have plenty of food." She looked directly at Ricky. "There are some drinks in the cooler too."

"We only came by to get Karri," Jeff said again.

"Karri isn't ready to go yet," Barry stated. "I'll bring her home when she is."

Just then, there was a commotion caused by several of the guys that had been standing beside the pickup when they arrived. There was a lot of laughing and giggling as a circle formed around a student from school.

"What's going on?" Anne asked.

"Oh, they're just having a little fun," Liz replied before hurrying over to get a better view.

"What kind of …" Christy didn't finish as she moved over to see what was going on.

It was soon obvious the boy had too much to drink and was sick. The boys surrounding him were all laughing at him.

When he tried to get up, he couldn't. He was looking around like he was having trouble focusing. "Hey, I know you. Aren't you that Jesus Girl."

Christy backed away from the scene with a sick feeling in her stomach. She remembered a speaker who had spoken to them the year before who had said that one of the things about drinking was that often your friends were the ones who laughed and made fun of you. He must have known what he was talking about. He had also talked about student's choices. Every one of them had to make them, and Christy knew drinking was a bad choice. Just being where she was made her feel she had made a bad choice.

*Please, Lord, forgive me for where I am.*

"Jeff, I would really like to go now," Christy told him as she found him talking to Anne.

"We can't leave Karri here like this," Jeff stated.

"You can't go yet," Liz declared. "The fun is just

beginning, and you will spoil everyone's fun if they have to leave to take you home."

"Liz, I don't belong here!" Christy responded.

"You need to loosen up some!" Liz laughed. "You think you're too good to drink with us?"

"I don't drink." Christy turned around and found Karri standing near her. "Karri, please go home with us."

"I don't want to go yet," Karri pleaded. "Please don't make a scene. I'm staying a little while longer. Barry said he would take me home."

"I can't stay, Karri," Christy answered. "I know my parents wouldn't approve. I'm not staying."

"Mommy and Daddy won't approve!" Liz jeered. "Here, Christy!" Liz pushed a beer bottle in Christy's face.

Christy reacted by slapping the bottle away, tipping the contents back on Liz.

"Now look what you've done!" Liz squealed in a shrill voice. "I should have known you were too much of a religious chick to enjoy life. If you're such a baby, what are you doing out here?"

"I'm asking myself that same question. When I find the answer, I'll be sure to let you know."

"Religious chick!" Sherri laughed. "That's a perfect name for her."

"What's the matter, Christy? You a chicken or something?" A tall boy Christy didn't even know declared from behind her. "You too afraid of getting in trouble with the parents?"

Sherri chuckled. "We knew you wouldn't fit in. Watch out for her halo, folks, some of that self-righteousness might get on you."

Some of the kids started making the sound like a chicken. "Bawwkkk! Bbbaawwwkkk! Bbbaaawwwkkk!"

Christy looked around at everyone. There were a lot of kids laughing at her. She wished she were anywhere other than where she was. She started walking. She would walk all the way home if she had too, but she wasn't staying here another moment.

"Christy! Wait!" Aaron was beside her. "I'll take you home." He took her arm and moved her toward where his jeep was parked.

"You can't leave yet Aaron!" Sherri shouted as she hurried along beside him. "You're letting her ruin everything! I knew we shouldn't have let her come out here!"

"Sherri, go back to the party!" Aaron told her. "I'm taking Christy home."

Jeff came up beside the jeep. "Don't worry about Karri, Anne and I will see she gets home safely."

"I wish she would come now," Christy said tears in her voice.

"Go on, Christy," Anne said, reassuring her. "We will be right behind you with Karri."

There was nothing else she could do. Aaron opened the passenger door on his jeep and helped Christy in. When he got in behind the steering wheel, he reached across her for the seat belt. She took the fastener and fastened herself in as she wondered how she had landed herself in this mess.

"Don't worry, Christy. Your friends will be okay."

"Thanks," She replied, glad he couldn't read her mind.

As they pulled away, Liz was up on one of the pickup

hoods, swaying to the loud music. She noticed it was only eleven by the clock on the dash of the jeep.

They rode to the main road in silence. "There is a jacket in the back if you're cold," Aaron said as he stopped before pulling out onto the highway.

Christy's teeth were chattering. "Please."

He left the jeep running and got out to get the jacket. When he got back in, he passed the jacket across to her. He waited while she unbuckled, put the jacket on, and then buckled herself back in.

"Don't let them make you feel bad about what happened back there." He studied her for a moment before smiling. "Besides, they are just jealous because they don't have a halo."

"It's not much fun being laughed at." Christy shrugged her shoulders as if it didn't matter, but it was obvious by the expression on her face that she cared what others thought of her.

"I would say it depends on what you're being laughed at about. Let them laugh. It takes guts to say no like you just did. Some of them wish they had the courage to do what you did."

"Oh, that's why they laughed at me and called me names?" Her eyes were bright with tears, but she couldn't help but smile at how he was trying so hard to lighten the moment.

"Well, are you?"

"Am I what?"

"Let me see a religious chick or a chicken?"

"I guess I am a little religious." Christy finally laughed. "I put myself in the position of being laughed at, and I feel I have let God down by being here. It's like the walk I was talking about the other day during our meeting. I don't want others to think that I talk the talk but don't walk the walk, if you know what I mean."

"I don't think they have any doubts on how you felt about their party, so don't let what they say or do hurt you," he replied with a smile of his own. "I think you kept your convictions and stood up for what you believe in."

"This wasn't your first time out here," Christy said, realizing it was a statement, not a question, once it was out of her mouth.

"No, I've been here a few times with Bill," Aaron answered. "I don't like drinking, but I have stood around with a bottle in my hand so I would fit in. No one noticed I kept the same drink in my hand all night. By the time I realized just how not cool I was being, it was too late to say I didn't want a beer. Now I realize it would have felt a whole lot better if I had just been myself and did what I felt like doing instead of what others expected me to do."

"I guess none of us like to be laughed at or thought of as different from the others around us," Christy stated. "My grandmother is always saying we never know what kind of influence we are having on others. If others see us do something we shouldn't, then they may think it's okay. I don't want anyone to think it's okay to drink or to do drugs."

"Most kids just want to fit in, and they think to do that they have to do what the crowd does. Like I said, it takes guts to stand up to the pressure, and you shouldn't feel bad or guilty about doing it back there."

"It's not that I feel bad about what I did back there.

I'm just sad that so many of those kids feel they have to do what everyone else is doing to fit in. I don't know about you, but I always thought if I was going to have fun, I wanted to know what I was doing. How would you know if you enjoyed something if you have no idea of what's going on?"

Aaron laughed. "I've never thought of it quite like that. I'll try and remember that the next time someone offers me a drink." He put the jeep in gear and pulled out onto the highway.

Christy was warm inside Aaron's jacket, and even though she felt bad about the others staying, she had a warm feeling inside when she remembered what Aaron said about it taking guts to stand up for your beliefs.

The drive to her house was over all too soon. She remembered she was supposed to be spending the night at Karri's so she would have to ring the doorbell to get in.

"I don't know how to thank you, Aaron," Christy said as she got out of the jeep. "I am just thankful you were there and willing to rescue me. I don't know what to say."

"I thought that was what friends were for?" Aaron replied.

"Thanks for being my friend, Aaron Smith."

"Good night, Christy." He told her as he placed his fingers under her chin and tilted her head up. For a minute, she thought he was going to kiss her. "Keep that head up, and don't let anyone make you feel bad about tonight."

"I will." She smiled back, a little disappointed when he removed his fingers.

"Good night."

Christy stood there while he got in his jeep to leave. He

didn't back out of the drive until Christy's grandmother opened the door to let her in.

"What are you doing home?" she asked, surprised to see her. "I thought you were spending the night at Karri's."

"A change of plans," Christy replied. "Mom already in bed?"

"Over an hour ago," Gran answered.

"Then I'll talk to her in the morning. I'll say goodnight," she said.

She hurried to her room not wanting to talk to anyone tonight. There would be plenty of explaining before she heard the last of tonight's little adventure, she was sure. At the moment, she just wanted to remember the time she had spent tonight with Aaron. She was glad he was her friend, but she couldn't help but wonder what it would have felt like if he had kissed her.

*Please let everything be all right, Lord. Let Karri, Anne, and Jeff get home safely. I am sorry that I let You down tonight by being out at the deer camp. I thank You that Aaron was there to bring me home. Even though I was made fun of I would rather stand against that behavior than to let You down by joining in. I Love You, Lord.*

# 12

Christy had just turned the vacuuming cleaner off when the phone started ringing downstairs. She still had not had a chance to talk to her mother about her change of plans from the night before. With only half of her Saturday morning chores finished, she knew it would be another hour before she could talk to her mother. She still had not decided exactly what she was going to say. There was no way she would lie to her mother, but that didn't mean telling her everything either. There were certain things that you just had to learn to deal with yourself, and surely this was one of them. A part of growing up was being able to deal with problems and accept responsibility without one's parents stepping in to solve them for you.

"Christy, it's for you!" she heard her mother call from downstairs.

Christy walked over to the phone beside her bed and lifted the receiver to her ear. After saying "hello," she heard her mother hang the downstairs phone up.

"Christy!" Anne's voice at the other end sounded excited. "You'll never believe what happened when Jeff and Dad went to get the car this morning."

"What?" Christy asked.

"It wasn't stuck!" Anne blurted.

"Wasn't stuck!" Christy exclaimed, her voice rising in volume at Anne's statement.

"Wasn't stuck." Anne repeated in a calmer voice.

"You're kidding me, right?" asked Christy, a frown deepening on her face.

"No, I'm serious. If you had been here and heard Dad when he got back home, you wouldn't doubt it either."

"But how is that possible?" Christy replied in an unbelieving voice.

"That's what Jeff and I have been asking each other," Anne responded. "Dad got Mr. Williams to take his wrecker out there to pull the car out after Jeff told him how badly stuck the car was. Jeff said when they got there, the car wasn't stuck. It wasn't even near a mud hole. And listen to this. There was no sign of any mud on it at all."

"How is that possible?" Christy questioned, sitting down on the side of her bed.

"I wish I knew." Anne returned.

"I don't understand how anyone could pull that off?"

"That's what dad kept asking Jeff and me. How could all the evidence just disappear like that? The car wasn't stuck. There wasn't any mud anywhere around where the car was parked. There wasn't any sign of mud on the car. Jeff also said there wasn't any sign the car had been washed, and there was a layer of dust on it from being driven out there."

"That's so weird."

"What's even more weird is Jeff didn't leave the keys in the car."

"Goodness, this sounds like something out of one of those sci-fi movies," Christy said. "Even worse, why would someone go to that amount of trouble?"

"It's certainly mysterious. I'm not sure I would believe it myself if I hadn't been there and witnessed it."

"We were there Anne," Christy said, assuring her. "I don't care what the evidence is this morning. We were stuck last night."

"That's reassuring. At present, Jeff and I are grounded for a month. All Dad will say is when you feel like telling me the truth about all of this, I will listen," Anne said disgustedly. "I think he thinks we were either drinking or high on something last night. Can you image if your own parent won't believe you? What everyone else is going to think?"

"The important thing is we aren't lying. We didn't do anything that we shouldn't other than go to that dumb party last night. Once the angry wears off, your parents are going to rethink all of this and know you are telling the truth."

"I sure hope so, but I don't think it will be anytime soon. Dad was pretty upset, especially since he had Mr. Williams go out there with them. Jeff said Dad was really embarrassed when Mr. Williams wouldn't stop laughing. Then he wouldn't take any money for taking them out there. Told Dad that now he had a real-live story that was funnier than anything he had heard in years."

"This doesn't make any sense to us, so can you image what the grown-ups think?"

"What makes me so mad is I know Liz is involved in all of this," Anne said. "Somehow we're going to get to the bottom of it."

"Even Liz can only do so much."

"Money talks," Anne replied. "She could have paid someone to help her pull this off. I'm not sure why anyone would be that sick. But I'm forgetting this is Liz we're talking about."

"None of this makes a lot of sense, but it's for sure someone planned for us to go out there last night. I don't think it was just a coincidence we were the ones that got the envelope to go see the light? The question is why?"

"We fell right into the trap."

"Okay. Let's say Liz set this all up. She tricked us, and we fell in with her plans. How are we going to prove anything?"

"I don't know yet, but I will," Anne said, assuring her. "I plan to get answers."

"What do you suggest we do first, Sherlock?" Christy giggled.

"How can you laugh at a time like this?" Anne demanded.

"It's either laugh or cry, and I don't exactly feel like crying."

"Listen, I have to get off the phone. I'm talking without permission as it is," Anne stated. "In the meantime, make a list of anything you can think of that was out of the ordinary last night."

"You mean like the fog?"

"What about the fog?" Anne asked.

"Didn't you notice the fog, smoke, or whatever was where we saw the light but wasn't anywhere else?" Christy asked.

"You called me Sherlock." Anne laughed. "I remember that now, but I guess it didn't register at the time. Things like that are exactly what I'm talking about."

"Before you go, what about Karri?" Christy asked.

"You think we're in trouble, she's in worse. She kept putting us off about leaving. I'm afraid she let Barry talk her into drinking. It was late before Jeff drove us all home. He wouldn't let Barry drive because he had too much to drink. Aaron followed us and dropped Jeff and me off at our house. We got into trouble because it was after one before we finally got home. I didn't spend the night at Karri's because her mom was so mad when she realized Karri had been drinking. I got my stuff and left."

"I'm surprised her mother hasn't called mine by now." Christy responded.

"Done worry. She will." Anne replied. "She blames us."

"Oh, boy."

"Well, I have to go. Don't forget to work on the list. We will compare notes at school Monday."

Shortly after hanging the phone up, the doorbell rang downstairs. Christy continued with cleaning the upstairs bathroom, knowing her mother would get the door. When she finished with the bathroom, she started on folding clothes. She was glad Anne had called and filled her in on what had happened after she left last night. She would have to tell her mother some of what had happened before she heard it from someone else. Looking up, she found her mother standing in her bedroom door. It was obvious she knew from the look on her mother's face.

"Why didn't you tell me about last night?" she asked in a quiet voice as she set Christy's overnight bag down on the bed.

"I was coming down to talk to you as soon as I finished putting the clothes up," Christy answered.

"Karri's mother just left, and she was upset with you." Christy's mother announced.

"Did she say why?" Christy asked.

"She said something about you, Anne, Jeff, and Ricky had brought Karri in last night and that all of you were drinking."

"We were not drinking!" Christy responded. "We got stuck."

"Stuck? Just where did you get stuck between here and the Parker house?"

"We did go to the Parker's house, but had to do this challenge and go and see the light before we joined the party out at Bill's camp."

"You didn't say anything about going to a party at a camp. You led me to believe the party was at Liz's house."

"The party did start out at Liz's house. They moved it to the camp later, but before we could go there we had to complete a challenge by going to see the light. Unfortunately, in the process we got stuck."

"I don't believe this. As many times as your dad and I have talked to you about being responsible, you can't say you weren't aware we would not approve of you going out there."

"Mom, will you let me explain?"

"I'm going to save you the trouble of telling your story twice because I know your grandmother is going to want to hear this too. She has gone to get her hair fixed but will be by for lunch. You can tell your story then."

"It's not as bad as it all sounds if you'll just listen," Christy said.

"So far it doesn't sound too promising," her mother said with skepticism in her voice.

"We weren't drinking. I promise," Christy insisted.

"Why would Karri's Mom think you were drinking? You know you can tell me anything."

Christy sighed. "Because Karri did drink."

"So there was drinking?"

"Only out at the camp. Will you let me explain?" Christy asked again knowing she wouldn't mention how the kids out at the camp were making fun and laughing at her.

"Just how did you get home?"

"Aaron Smith brought me home."

"So, you didn't even come home with who you left with. Just go to your room and stay there until your grandmother gets home."

"But Mom…"

"Young Lady …"

"There is just one problem, Mom," Christy replied louder.

"And that is?"

"I'm in my room."

There was a moment of silence as Mrs. Rivers looked around. "Your dad would be so disappointed. I have a feeling he isn't going to be so happy about this."

"Mom don't be so upset with me. We really didn't do anything wrong but did not come home when we left Liz's house. And I can assure you, if we had it to do over again, we would never have gone to the party to start with."

"It's a little too late for regrets. I'll call you down when Gran gets here."

"This is so unfair."

"You should have considered the consequences of your actions."

"Is it alright for me to call Karri?" Christy requested as her mother went to leave.

"No, that seems to be one of the consequences. Mrs. Taylor does not want you to talk or go anywhere near her daughter."

"I haven't done anything that would cause Mrs. Taylor to say that."

"She must think differently. Because that is what she said when she brought your overnight bag home."

Christy was stunned. It was all so unfair. She didn't want to blame the unfairness on Karri's mom nor on her own, but it certainly was tempting. Grown-ups were always telling their kids to listen, but sometimes they didn't practice what they preach.

Christy sat down in the window seat to wait for her summons downstairs. She hoped Gran and her mother would keep an open mind until she explained the whole story. She wondered if Gran would be as upset as her mother.

*Thank You, Lord, for being my friend. I seem to be on my own here. I am truly sorry that all of this happened. Help me get back on track and make this okay somehow. I Love You.*

# 13

Taking out her *Bible*, Christy studied her Sunday school lesson while waiting on her mother to call her down stairs. She was just completing the question-and-answer part of the lesson when her mother called up the stairs for her to come down. She was a little nervous about confronting her mother and grandmother after her mother's reaction. They usually listened to her problems and gave good advice, but she wasn't sure what to expect.

All the way downstairs, she kept telling herself, *This time would be no different. They will listen. They will be fair. They just had to be.*

She entered the kitchen a little apprehensive to find her Gran sitting at the breakfast table reading the daily newspaper with a cup of coffee in her hand. Carrie Rivers was a petite woman with a sense of humor that most people noticed right off. She had beautiful white hair now, but it had once been the dark-brown shade as Christy's and they shared the same deep-blue eye color. There was enough similarity in their features that there was no mistaking they were related. Where her father and mother were both medium height, Christy had gotten her petite build from her grandmother. Today she looked much younger dressed in faded blue jeans and a blue T-shirt. Christy was glad to see her looking so relaxed.

"Good morning, Christy," she said as Christy entered the room. There was a twinkle in her blue eyes.

"Hey, Gran," Christy returned the greeting walking over to give her a big hug.

She got a glass out of the cabinet before going over to the refrigerator for ice. After pouring a glass of tea, she took a seat on one of the stools at the counter that separated the kitchen from the breakfast area.

"What's this your mother has been telling me about your little adventure last night?" Gran asked, wasting no time.

"Where do you want me to start?" Christy asked.

"At the beginning is usually the best place," her mother answered.

So Christy spent the next thirty minutes telling her mother and grandmother about the night-before happenings. Her Gran had even laughed a couple of times during the narrating. She was glad she found some humor in their exciting experience. She could tell her mother didn't. They listened intently as she told how Jeff and his father had found the car unstuck that morning. She only omitted a few details like the dance with Aaron and their conversation when he was bringing her home. She also left out the part about the drinking at the camp and that she had been made fun of. She finished with Aaron bringing her home when they got to the deer camp to get Karri and she wouldn't leave.

"You did the right thing by coming on home," Gran said. "I know Aaron. He works at the paper and seems like a fine young man. I would like to thank him for seeing you got home safely."

"He really is nice," Christy replied. "I wouldn't have let him bring me home if I had thought I wouldn't have been safe with him."

"I'm glad you came on home too, but you should have made Karri and Anne come with you," her mother said, stirring soup on the stove.

"Who was supervising this party?" Gran asked.

Christy didn't want to lie, but she didn't want to be a tattletale either. She finally said, "I didn't see any adults, but I wasn't there very long."

"There probably wasn't any adult supervision out there," her mother said. "That was one of the things Karri's mother was so upset about."

"Mary, that is hardly Christy's fault."

"Still, she shouldn't have left Karri out there. I would be upset with Karri if she had left Christy."

"Mom, I couldn't make Karri leave since she didn't want to. Anne and Jeff stayed with her, and they said they would see she got home safely. They got in a lot of trouble with their parents because they stayed with her."

"All of you should have left together," she repeated.

"All of us didn't," Christy stated the obvious.

"You should have insisted they leave with you," her mother continued.

"Let it go, Mary." Gran gaze was on Christy's face.

"She did what she felt she had to do at the time. If Karri didn't want to leave, there was little she could do to make her."

"What's my punishment?" Christy asked the dreaded question.

"Seems to me you may already have a punishment. Karri's mother has requested you stay away and not talk to her. You are to honor that request," her mother replied.

"But Mom!" Christy cried. "I didn't do anything!"

"By going where you know you shouldn't have been is something, and maybe the reason you're faced with this situation."

"Just what would you have done Mom?"

"Christy, you know not to use that tone of voice with your mother!" Gran was no happier than her mom about the whole occurrence, but she was right. She should not talk in that tone toward her mother.

"I'm sorry, but what else could I have done? I could have stayed out there and been in even more trouble. If I had come home and told on my friends last night, they would feel I had betrayed them today. I'd be classified as a snitch, and no one would want to be my friend."

As far as Christy was concerned, she had done all she could, and if she had it all to do over again, she would have done the same.

"You could have told us," her mother said quietly.

"Then what? You would have called both Karri's and Anne's moms, and I still would be in trouble with them. They'd all think I was a tattletale. It's bad enough everyone thinks I'm not normal or something."

"What do you mean?"

"Please, this is my problem. Can't you give me some space and let me try and solve it myself?"

"Just remember if you need to talk, we're here for you," Gran reminded her.

"I do know that. That means a lot to me. I just need to try and find my own solution this time,"

They both nodded.

"Then we will let you work this out yourself, but you have to honor Mrs. Taylor's request."

"I won't try and talk to Karri, but I won't ignore her if she tries to talk to me. She is still my friend."

"Fair enough, but she has to make the first move," her mother stated. "And Christy, I'm not upset with you for coming home when you found yourself in the situation you found yourself in last night."

"I know why you are upset with me, Mom. What you don't understand is I'm upset with myself that I trusted Liz again with wanting to be friends. I will assure you I've learned by my mistake, and I won't be repeating it.

"That is good to know," her mother stated. "Now, let's try this soup."

After lunch, she spent an hour practicing basketball in the driveway. She went inside and grabbed her laptop to finish up homework for the following Monday for her history journal. She had been watching the news on both president candidates and was enjoying commenting on the election. It was sad to read and hear some of the things that were being said and done, but that seemed to be politics.

She especially wanted to talk to Anne and Karri but knew she would have to be patient and let them contact her. It was evening before she got a chance to sit down and watch a movie with her mother and grandmother. The evening was so different than the night before. Why did life have to be so complicated?

*Thank You, Lord, for my relationship with You. I choose this day to be positive, even when the circumstances of last night are negative. I pray for my friends that they can work things out with their parents so they will not be in trouble. I'm very thankful that Mom and Gran listened to what happened and are not mad at me. I Love You, Lord*

# 14

**C**hristy awoke on Monday morning to the sound of rain on the roof. She lifted her head and glanced at the window. It was darker than usual outside, and she found herself hoping this wasn't an omen of what kind of day was ahead. The weather may have been the first ominous warning of the day. The second came on reaching school and finding the story about the car had already spread like wildfire. Whispers followed Christy down the hall to the gym where everyone was since it was raining outside. She sought out Anne in the bleachers. Jeff and Ricky were the only ones seated near her. Ordinarily they would be talking and laughing with their friends.

"Everyone knows," Christy stated as she sat down beside Anne.

"You don't know the half of it," Anne replied. "My parents have gotten so many phone calls this weekend that they are thinking about having an unlisted number put in."

"No one is sitting with us because it's hard to sit with someone if you want to talk about them." Jeff's voice sounding sarcastic. "You would think we have committed some sort of crime instead of just getting a car stuck."

Just then someone called out, "Hey, Jeff, what were you on Friday night?"

"We heard you thought you were stuck, so I want to be sure not to use whatever you took." Laughter rang out around them.

Christy felt her cheeks burn as she heard the laughter rising around them. All the kids were looking at them and laughing. She could tell by the looks on the others' faces that they were embarrassed as well.

Jeff ignored the comments, staring straight ahead. His expression was serious, nothing at all like his usual grinning one, offering no clue to what was going through his mind.

"I'm sick of this already," Ricky commented.

"You had better learn to ignore it because it's probably going to get worse before it gets better," Jeff stated with a disgusted look on his face.

"But we haven't done anything wrong," Anne replied.

"I know, but no one believes what really happened," Jeff answered. "We didn't have to do anything wrong."

"Lots of students were there. They know we are telling the truth," Christy stated.

"Not really," Jeff replied. "No one actually saw us stuck but us."

"What about Aaron?" Christy asked. "He came and picked us up."

"He didn't see us stuck."

"He saw the mud all over you and Jeff," Christy suggested. "Couldn't we use him as a witness?"

"That's an idea!" Anne exclaimed. "Everyone would believe him."

"It doesn't matter. The point is they didn't believe us," Jeff said. "Now I don't care what anyone thinks."

Christy sighed. She knew Jeff did care but understood exactly where he was coming from. There didn't seem to be a whole lot they could do about any of it for the time being. They would just have to wait until something else came along to be the center of everyone's attention. For now, they seem to be the topic.

"They can't say anything worse than they already have," Ricky offered optimistically as the bell rang, indicating the start of the school day.

They found he was wrong. As the day progressed, the stories grew more and more outrageous with each telling. After listening to one more tall tale, Christy found herself trying to explain the truth. After being interrupted a couple of times by laughter from the rest of the class, she finally gave up, especially when one of the students said, "Oh, that's right. You were with them. Give us a firsthand report. That is, if you can remember what it is." They could think what they wanted.

To make matters worse, Karri wasn't speaking to her. She had passed her in the hall twice, and each time when their eyes met, Karri had looked quickly away. Perhaps she felt bad about what happened Friday night. Still, Christy couldn't understand why she was acting this way. Every time she saw her, she had been with Liz and Sherri. It just didn't make sense. Karri had never liked Liz. Why would she decide all of a sudden to be friends with her?

It was really beginning to get old by last block, and they were on their way to basketball practice. Once out on the court, Christy forgot the problems that had followed her around all day and enjoyed playing basketball. Warm-ups went much as they always did, but almost immediately once they started scrimmaging, there was something different in the air.

For one thing, Coach Thomas moved Karri to Christy's position and put Christy on the second team. Karri wasn't as quick as Christy or as good an outside shooter, but the other players were passing her the ball more, and they were working together as a team. It was plain this wasn't the first time they had set up and run the plays they were using.

Although they made several good plays, Christy could tell the second team was no match for the first. Their defense was a lot better than their offense. Since Christy and Tonya were the only shooters, it was easier for the first team to double-team them, and they had a hard time scoring. Christy found herself very discouraged by the end of practice.

After a pep talk, Coach Thomas dismissed the rest of the team but said, "Rivers, Taylor, I want to see you in my office." She walked ahead of them off the court.

Christy and Anne looked at each other before following her.

"What do you think she wants?" Anne asked.

"Friday's incident."

"I hope you're wrong."

"I'm not," Christy replied with conviction.

Christy felt churning sensations in her stomach like she got before having to do something that made her nervous. Surely Coach Thomas wouldn't take them off the team. Wouldn't she have done that at the beginning of practice? For sure, it had to be about what had happened this weekend.

It didn't take Coach Thomas long to come to the point. Once seated behind her desk, she placed her fingers together and waited till both girls were focused on her before stating her opinion, "I thought I had made myself perfectly clear the first day here what kind of behavior I expected from girls who play on my team. You are role models, and as such, you must live up to the high expectations that are required. I've heard a lot of talk this weekend and today at school. I know not all of it could possibly be true, or you wouldn't have been able to come to school today. But, I do want to know if there is any truth in what I'm hearing."

"We did get stuck Friday night," Anne assured her.

"Christy?" Coach Thomas asked.

"We really did, Coach Thomas."

"I don't appreciate being lied to, girls," Coach Thomas answered in a quiet voice. "I am really disappointed in both of you. I didn't want to believe what I have heard all weekend. Were you drinking or using drugs?"

"Absolutely not!" Christy said looking her straight in the eye. "I'm willing to take a drug test to prove it, if it comes to that."

"Me too," Anne added.

"What about the car not being stuck when your father went to get it? Can you explain that?"

"I don't know," Anne answered.

"Well, I don't know either. You're both good players, but I have had a couple of the players come to talk to me about this incident and the image your actions place on the team. As role models, I'm very disappointed in both of you. After talking to several teachers who assure me neither of you have ever done anything like this before, I feel placing you on probation for now is better than kicking you completely off the team."

"On probation!" cried Christy. "What for?"

"Because I will not put up with deplorable behavior by any member of this team," Coach Thomas told them. "This past weekend's behavior meets that standard. By putting you on probation you will remain on the team unless any more incidents like this occur."

"That's so unfair!" Anne exclaimed. "We aren't guilty of anything but getting stuck."

"You know it is more than that. Every girl on this team knows about your actions Friday night. There has to be some sort of punishment, or someone else will think if you get away with this, it's okay to behave in this manner. No matter what you think, your behavior does reflect on this team. I will not tolerate being lied to."

"Everyone says we are lying," Anne said.

"I've checked the evidence out myself," Coach Thomas replied. "After two of the girls came and talked to me, I talked to others about this. Anne, your father was one of those I talked to."

"So my father told you I was lying."

"It seems the evidence points in that direction."

Christy was so mad that she thought she would explode. Liz was really to blame for all of this, yet she gets off free and clear. Liz and Sherri had to be the two girls that Coach Thomas kept referring to.

"Just one question, Coach Thomas," Christy stated. "Was Liz and Sherri the two who talked to you about this?"

"I've tried to ignore some of the animosity between Liz and you because I think you both could be valuable members of this team. Yes, Liz came to me with concerns about this weekend, but the other person wasn't Sherri. It was Karri Tucker."

Christy felt she had been slapped. Karr had done this. Her friend the one who knew how important playing on the team was to her had done this. She just couldn't believe it. Not Karri.

"I'm giving you fair warning, I'm not ignoring anything that will cause friction for this team. You can both work together and make this team a real team or …"

She didn't have to finish the statement Christy clearly understood her meaning. She was infuriated. Coach Thomas thought she was jealous of Liz. She didn't believe them about being stuck. Nothing they said would make any difference at this point.

Christy stood up to leave. "If you say I'm on probation because I used bad judgment, then I won't argue with you about that because I did. I won't argue with you about the other, I can see you already had your mind made up when you invited us in here."

I'm sorry you feel that way," Coach Thomas replied. "I will say I'm disappointed in both of you."

"I could say the same," Christy answered.

"Don't get smart with me."

"May we go?" Christy asked.

"You understand that probation means …"

"We're off the team if any more problems occur." Christy finished.

"Is that understood?"

"We understand." Christy couldn't believe this was happening.

*Listening to gossip was one thing, but getting kicked off the team because of it was the pits. Even worse is your best friend telling the lie. But why?*

"May we go now?" Christy asked again.

"Yes, you may go."

"First my parents and now this," Anne said with tears in her voice. "I feel that I'm in the middle of a nightmare and I can't wake up. It hurts so much that so many people that I care about don't believe what really happened."

"You have to give Liz credit. She really planned a good prank. "What's so unbelievable is that it is working. How is she getting Karri to go along with this?"

"What are we going to do?" Anne asked.

"Stay out of trouble for one thing." Christy replied. "I didn't work all summer to be kicked off this team. As bad as I would like to give a certain person a taste of her own medicine, I don't think we can afford to get into any more trouble. Besides, she would get too much enjoyment out of us getting kicked off the team to let that happen."

"So what do we do?" Anne repeated her question.

"We're going to act like everything is fine for now."

"What will that prove?"

"It won't prove anything, but it will keep Liz from getting what she wants."

"That's us off the team," Anne muttered. "The thing is, Liz will have a backup plan if this one fails."

"For sure."

"I'm not sure I'm going to be a very good actress," Anne added.

"Here comes your chance to find out," Christy stated as Karri came out of the dressing room with Liz and Sherri and started down the hallway in their direction.

Karri didn't try to speak to them but kept walking as if she didn't know them as they met in the hallway. The looks on Liz and Sherry's faces were ones of pure glee.

"Some people just can't seem to stay out of trouble," Liz said as they moved past. The sound of laughter followed them out the door.

"Come on, Anne." Christy headed toward the dressing room. "Let's get dress and out of here."

"How do you do it?"

"Do what?" Christy asked.

Anne shook her head. "You're being so calm about this. I'm so mad I can't think straight, and you're calm as can be. What's your secret?"

"Believe me, I'm not that calm. I'm practicing counting to ten before opening my mouth. My grandmother is always telling me don't speak when your heart is disturbed. So I'm trying really hard to follow her advice."

"I think she has the right idea."

"She's the greatest. It's like she always knows just what to say when I need her to say it. She would probably tell me right now not to let my tongue run away with me and say something I may regret and can't take back. She's always saying things like, 'Be careful of the words you speak today, for tomorrow you might have to eat them.'"

"I have a feeling we better not speak any words for a while because I don't think what I would like to say right now would taste too good," Anne replied.

They both were laughing when they opened the dressing room door.

"The whole thing is so unfair!" Tonya was saying as they came in the door.

"Coach must not have been to upset with the two of you if you can still laugh." Mia said.

Christy shrugged. "She had to say something. After all we are supposed to be role models."

"It's just so unfair!" Tonya protested again. "They somehow planned all of this. Did you know they practiced together on Saturday and Sunday afternoons?  Not only that, but Liz told Coach Thomas that we didn't want to practice with them over the weekend."

Christy found Karri's part in all this so unbelievable and so out of character. Even if all of this was unfair, she knew better than to complain. It would do little good. And getting kicked off the team wasn't worth fighting back.

"I don't know of anything we can do about it."

"You should be playing with the first team. We all know that," stated Tonya.

"Don't you like me playing with you?" Christy teased.

"Oh no! It's not that," explained Tonya. "We like you on our team just fine. It's just that Liz seems to be up to her old tricks again like last year. I thought this year was going to be different, but she is getting away with it again."

"She needs some of her own medicine," Mia replied. "Hey! I know! I know!"

"You know what?" Tonya asked.

"Think about this," Mia replied. "What would happen if in two weeks at the purple-and-white game if the second team just happened to beat the first team?" Her eyes were sparkling when she finished stating her idea. "I can see her now!"

"You're dreaming Mia," Anne responded. "Even with Christy and Tonya on our side, we still have a long way to go before we could beat them."

"What do you think, Christy?" Tonya asked. "Could we beat them?"

"Hope see the invisible, feels the intangible, and achieves the impossible," Christy answered, pulling her shoes off.

"Wow! Where did that come from?" Tonya demanded.

"I read it somewhere," Christy tried to smile.

"Is that a yes?" Mia questioned.

Christy looked at her friends and wished she could encourage them in the idea but knew this would get her kicked off the team. They were showing a faith that she didn't know if she shared. "Coach Thomas would not like it, and she might think we are trying to divide the team more."

"If Coach Thomas can't see the team is divided already, maybe we need to take up a collection and buy her a pair of glasses," Tonya responded.

"You going to be the one to give them to her?" Christy asked.

"Not me!"

"I don't think she would appreciate the gesture," Christy stated with confidence. She didn't tell them how she knew, but when Anne's eyes met hers she knew her friend understood.

"Couldn't we at least try?" Mia pleaded.

Christy shook her head. "I don't think we should." She could tell Tonya and Mia were both disappointed, but she couldn't erase the memory of Coach Thomas's warning earlier. She wasn't ready to give up her dream of having a place on this year's team.

*Lord, I am sad that Karri seems to be against me along with Liz. No one believes us about what happened. Please help us to stay out of more trouble with Coach Thomas and not do anything that will get us kicked off the team. Please continue to watch over Dad and Sam. Keep them safe. I love You.*

# 15

During scrimmage the next day, everyone played more aggressively than Christy could ever remember. She had been fouled more than anyone. It was like the first team was out for blood, and it seemed to be hers. She had plenty of bruises and floor burns to prove it. At the beginning of practice, everything seems to go as most practices did with nothing out of the ordinary.  Once scrimmaging started, they were up and down the court, trading goal for goal.

Then everything changed when she intercepted a pass from Sherri by moving in front of Liz. She caught the ball, turned, and dribbled back toward the other goal. When she reached center court, she passed to Tonya, who was running toward the basket Liz several steps behind her. Tonya caught the ball, bounced it once, and laid it up against the backboard for two points.

"You were just lucky," Liz said as she went back down the court past Christy.

After Christy stole the ball again, the whole tempo of the practice changed. Just moments after the last steal, Christy hit the floor as Sherri charged driving toward the basket. Christy felt pain where her hip and elbow hit the floor.

Anne was bending over her. "Are you okay?" She extended a hand to help her up.

Christy took her hand and let her pull her up. "Sure."

Several minutes later when she drove in for a layup instead of blocking the shot, Liz knocked her flying. Again she found herself getting up off the floor. The look on Liz's face told her that this was no accident but was intentional.

Still she knew she couldn't afford to retaliate. Coach Thomas blew the whistle and called a foul, letting her know that she thought Liz had just got overaggressive and didn't intend to hit her.

The second team had received the ball, and they brought the ball back into play. This time Mia drove to the basket and charged Sherri, knocking her to the floor. Again, the whistle blew and a foul was called.

"You can't go through the guard, girls. Now come on and use your heads," Coach Thomas told all of them.

The next few minutes, they did settle down and play without fouling until again Christy with her quickness striped the ball from Sherri's hands. One moment Sherri had the ball; the next Christy was dribbling the other way. This time she passed to Anne under the basket, and she laid the ball up for two more points. They were now four points ahead of the first team.

Christy moved back into position as Sherri brought the ball back down the court. She worried Sherri enough that she was making bad passes, and this time Mia grabbed a ball intended for Karri. As soon as Christy saw she had the ball, she had taken off down the court. Mia threw a pass that she caught, bounced the ball twice, and laid the ball up against the backboard for two more points.

The second team had not been practicing together, but it was like they had each play mapped out before it took place. When Sherri brought the ball down the court this time, they all sagged on defense and wouldn't let them get the ball into Liz. Sherri wasn't a good outside shooter, so Christy only went out on her when she got in close enough to score. Sherri finally passed off to Karri, who shot the ball, hit the rim, and bounced off into Tonya's hands.

Tonya passed to Christy, who quickly zipped a pass up court to Mia. She sent it back to Christy, and she drove by her guard. She was able to get a bounce pass off to Tonya when Liz picked her up. Tonya went up with the ball, but she shot too hard, and the ball bounced up.

Christy moved in for the rebound. She leaped, felt the ball on her fingertips. Then the next thing she knew, she was meeting the floor once again. She lay there, trying to get her breath. She felt pain all over, and she tried to get up. But couldn't for a moment.

Finally she rolled over on her side. Tonya, Anne, and Mia were bending over her.

"Are you all right?" Tonya asked.

Then the Coach was there. "Move back and let her have some air. Are you okay?"

Christy took Anne and Tonya's hands and let them help her up.

"I'm sorry," Liz was saying, but the look in her eyes let Christy know she was anything but sorry.

"Save it, Liz. We both know you're not," Christy said without thinking.

She instantly knew she had made a huge mistake. Coach Thomas had heard.

"Davey, take Rivers' place. She motioned for Christy to take a seat.

After the ball was put back into play, Coach Thomas stared at Christy thoughtfully. "You really dislike Liz, don't you?"

Christy didn't know how to answer. She didn't want to be untruthful, but she didn't think Coach Thomas would appreciate her telling her how she really felt about Liz.

So instead she replied, "My feelings toward her simply don't come into this."

"I think they do. What's more, I think your attitude is influencing other members on this team."

Christy looked at the coach, genuinely surprised she had made the comment. "You think all of this is my fault?"

"Whether you are doing it intentionally or not, I don't know, but it has to stop. Our team doesn't stand a chance of a good season if this continues. In fact, I will not allow this to continue. I thought I had made myself clear about this, but I still see a problem." She paused a moment before adding. "You've got to get along while you are on the court. I can't tell you how to act or behave anywhere else, but I will not tolerate it here."

"You've shared this concern with Liz too?"

Coach Thomas just stared at her for a moment like lost for words.

Christy wanted to let her know about the sort of trouble Liz was causing, but she could tell it would fall on deaf ears. She felt she would be called jealous of Liz or something again if she said anything else. So, she gave in to the useless effort to share the blame. If the coach couldn't see what was going on there wasn't much she could do about it. She lost a little more of her confidence of getting to play on the team and seeing playing time.

When she was allowed back on the court, she moved through the rest of the practice like a robot. Her mind wasn't really on what she was doing, and she found it extremely hard to put any heart into the practice. During the summer and all the long hours she had spent working, she had never considered the possibility of failure once she had set her goal.

By the end of practice, she felt more discouraged than she would ever have dreamed possible. For the first time, she couldn't help wondering was all that hard work in vain.

"Hey, is everything okay?" Anne asked, looking concerned at her friend's down cast face as she ran up beside her after practice.

"Sure," Christy replied.

"That was a pretty bad fall." Anne continued before Christy cut her off.

"I'm fine."

"Liz did it on purpose. I heard Sherri congratulated her on it going back down the court."

A resigned look crossed Christy's face as she said calmly, "It doesn't matter. Coach Thomas thinks I'm the problem."

"You?"

"Yeah," Christy answered, sick of the whole thing. "Let's just forget about it."

"Forget about it?" Anne replied. "But Christy…."

"Just drop it, Anne," Christy repeated. "It really doesn't matter right now."

"Are you sure you're okay?"

"I'm fine," Christy said. At the same time, she felt a twinge of pain in her hip where she had hit the floor. The pain in her hip didn't come close to comparing to the pain she felt in the proximity of her heart at that moment.

Anne made a face. "Sure, but you don't sound like yourself. Are you sure you didn't hit your head or something?"

"Or something," Christy finally laughed bitterly.

She rubbed her hip where it was hurting. In fact, her whole body was smarting from the spills she had taken. She had received bruises and floor burns before. To play basketball, you had to be tough. That was part of the sport. But she couldn't help thinking you were supposed to receive your war scares from your opponents, the opposing team, not your teammates.

Whether Coach Thomas wanted to see it or not, Liz's hostility toward her was real. Right at this moment, Christy really didn't know what to do about it. As she entered the locker room, all around her, her teammates were laughing and exchanging gossip. She didn't feel up to the lighthearted atmosphere, so she just changed her shoes. She would shower when she got home.

"Christy, you look so exhausted," Liz commented with a laugh. "Or is it you look sore?"

Several girls chuckled at this, but Christy didn't comment, knowing exactly what Liz was up to.

"What? Cat got your tongue?" Sherri laughed.

Christy smiled. She might have got licked out on the court today, but she would win this one by not retaliating. "I'll live." With that, she had walked out of the locker room without saying anything else.

Karri was standing near the door, and their eyes met. Karri looked like she wanted to say something but remained silent as Christy left.

The worst part of the day came a few minutes later. After going back through the building to get her books, she was on her way out the door to go to the jeep. While waiting to cross the street, she had seen Liz and Sherri hanging out of Aaron's jeep as he drove by. For some reason, she remembered her grandmother saying either things will get better or they will get worse, but for sure they won't remain the same. This feeling of defeat must be what she meant by things could get worse.

*Please, Lord, don't let this get any worse than it already is.*

Aaron had not been to anymore of the meetings for the Christian fellowship; nor had he shown up on the morning of See You at the Pole. He was at church most Sundays but still didn't come to any of the extra activities. Bobby had continued to come to their meetings and was a regular in singing with them on Sunday nights. She continued to pray for Aaron, but after the day she had, she wasn't sure he was any closer to knowing God than he was the first day she met him.

Later that evening as Christy sat at her desk, a frown on her face, she stared at the blank page in front of her. She had an essay to write for history, "An American Symbol." The subject was to go along with their word of the week "patriotism." The essay wasn't due until Friday, but she wanted to get started on it early so she would have time to revise it if she need to.

When Mr. Reynolds begin talking about patriotism on Friday of the week before, Christy had instantly known what symbol she wanted to use to do her paper on, the American flag. She sighed heavily as the paper remained blank in front of her. She knew the thoughts that she wanted to express, but she couldn't seem to get them down on paper. How could she write so others would feel the pride, respect, hopes, and dreams that the flag had represented for people of the United States down through the years? It was a symbol of freedom that many had given their lives for. It wasn't enough that she felt these thoughts; she wanted her paper to help others to feel them too. She had ideas on how to tie in patriotism, but she was having problems writing them down.

Closing the notebook, she would work on her paper later. She had too many thoughts running through her head to be able to get what she wanted to say down.

*Lord, this has been a really frustrating day, and I feel a little defeated. I am sorry that I am letting You down, but I just feel so mad at Liz most of the time. She seems to be getting away with everything, and Coach believes I am the problem and not her. Please help me to do what is right and not ruin my chances to play on the team. Karri looks so unhappy, but I can't talk to her right now. Would You please work on getting whatever is going on with her straightened out? Aaron has hardly spoken to me in the past couple of weeks. I see him at school and at church, but we haven't had any time to talk. I pray that he will come to know You, Lord. Thanks for watching out for my dad and Sam. May they get to come home soon. I love You.*

# 16



"Once you say you're going to settle for second, that's what happens to you in life." The daily thought had been read in the bulletin earlier in the day, and it had repeatedly played over and over in Christy's mind all day. Was that what she was doing when she tried to banish the thoughts of banding together with her teammates to beat the first team at the purple-and-white game? Although Tonya and Mia had said nothing more about Mia's idea, she knew they were hopeful that something would change her mind.

So far she had stayed out of further trouble after Coach Thomas's last warning, but it was getting harder and harder to keep her mouth shut. Liz was really throwing her weight around as captain of the team. She was even picking on the first team, especially on Karri. Was Liz staging something else? Christy didn't know, but she could feel something was going on there. She just couldn't figure out what.

Sherri brought the ball down the court, passing to Karri on the wing. Karri shot, but the ball hit the rim and bounced up.

"Rebound!" Coach Thomas shouted to the players.

Liz grabbed the rebound and put it back up and in. "That's it!"

Most of the instructions were for the first team. Christy felt it didn't matter too much what the second team did as long as the first team didn't make too many mistakes. She felt herself moving through the practice with a half-hearted effort. Liz intercepted a pass intended for her because she was not where she was supposed to be.

"Set it up!" Coach Thomas shouted once again. She seemed to be shouting a lot today.

A moment later, the sound of a whistle stopped the play altogether. "That was awful!" She told them pausing for a moment. "There's no room for sloppy playing on this team. Poor passing, careless ball handling, and little effort only develop poor habits that will show up later in a game. Rivers! Where are you today? That was the third time that you failed to move into position letting Liz steal the ball right out of your hands."

Christy didn't have an answer. The smile on Liz's face didn't make her feel any better.

"Woods, take Rivers' place. Sit down and watch. Maybe Woods wants to play more than you do."

Christy carefully kept her feelings to herself. As she walked over and took a seat, she could have cried in frustration, but she would not let her teammates see her tears.

"I would never have taken you for a quitter," Coach

Thomas said quietly a few minutes later as she stood near where Christy sat on the bench.

Christy looked up at her with surprise. "I'm not," She replied in a low tone.

"Aren't you?"

"We all have bad days," Christy answered, fighting to keep tears at bay.

"This is more than a few bad days," Coach Thomas stated. "Look out there on the floor. They look nothing like they usually do when you're out there, giving it all you've got. When you play sloppy, they do too."

"I'm sorry."

"I don't want you to be sorry. I want you to show me each time you get out on that court just how much you love the game and how badly you want to play. You can be more than just a pretty good player, if you want it badly enough. You and I both know it. I just hope you aren't going to give up without a fight."

"I don't intend to!"

"Then how about getting out there and playing like you want to be on this team?" Coach Thomas said as she blew her whistle once more. She put Christy back in.

The rest of the practice, the second team redeemed themselves by playing much better. Christy noticed that Coach Thomas was right. When she played hard, the rest of her teammates played hard with her. She would have to remember that. It was one thing to let herself down, but she was letting them down too when she didn't give her best.

Liz rebounded a missed shot by Tonya, but when she went to pass the ball out to Sherri, Christy, in a position to intercept the ball, automatically jumped to receive the pass. She caught the pass, dribbled twice back toward the basket, leaped, and sank a long jump shot.

"Way to go!" shouted Tonya, running up to give Christy a high five. You would have thought she was the one who made the play. The grin was so wide on her face.

Coach Thomas blew her whistle. She motioned for the girls to sit on the floor while she gave them one of her pep talks. She pointed out some of the mistakes they were making and then told them what she expected them to do to correct them. After reminding them that it was just a week and a half until the purple-and-white game, she finally dismissed them for the day.

Liz was her usual bossy self in the locker room, so much so Christy had to bite her tongue to keep from telling her to shut up. She also noticed Karri didn't seem to be speaking to Liz or Sherri, and there were dark circles under her eyes as well as a sad expression in them.

"What about Aaron?" Liz asked.

Christy hadn't been listening to the conversation around her until she heard Aaron's name. She wanted to ask what about him, but she couldn't very well do that.

"He said he might be able to go. He would have to let me know tomorrow," Sherri replied.

"Great! I just love to double date," Liz said loudly.

Christy was sure they were making sure she heard them.

"Karri, we'll have to check and see if Barry can go with us," Liz added.

"That's all right, Liz. I'm going to my grandmother's this weekend. I can't."

Liz chuckled. "Maybe next time."

"Yeah, maybe next time," Karri answered, showing little enthusiasm for the idea. Christy definitely felt there was some tension in the air. She wished Karri would talk to her, but she had promised her mother she wouldn't make the first move.

"Do you have your history assignment done yet?" Anne asked as they left the dressing room.

"Not really. I know what I want to write about. It's just not ready to flow yet."

Anne groaned as she shook her head at Christy. She always seemed to be able to get writing assignments finished while everyone else was struggling with what to write theirs on.

"You would," Anne exclaimed. "I don't even know yet what I'm going to write about."

Christy and Anne walked back through the building to their lockers for their books.

"Do you think Sherri has a date with Aaron?" Anne asked.

"Who knows," Christy said as she got her math book out of her locker.

"Karri didn't seem excited to go out with Barry again," Anne added.

"You noticed that too," Christy agreed.

"What do you think?" Anne asked.

"There's something wrong there. I just don't know what."

"Want to go to Sawyers?"

Christy sighed, "Wish I could but I've got to go to tutoring. I missed several problems on my math quiz yesterday. I can't wait till we have a test to find out what I'm doing wrong."

"I'll see you tomorrow then."

When Christy arrived in Mr. Coleman's room for tutoring, she found Aaron there ahead of her.

"Hey, Christy, you need some help in math too?"

"The last two problems on the quiz yesterday were way over my head."

"Mine too."

Mr. Coleman arrived just then and was ready to get down to working on some of the math problems they were having trouble solving. Less than thirty minutes later Christy and Aaron both understood what they were doing wrong and were ready to leave.

As they walked out together, Aaron asked Christy, "Do you need a ride home?"

"I'm in the jeep."

"Would you like to stop by Sawyers on the way?"

"I don't have any money with me. I will have to run by my house."

"That's okay. My treat."

"Then I would love to," Christy replied.

Aaron had to walk further to his jeep than Christy, so she put her books in the back of the jeep before climbing in and bucking up. She couldn't believe that Aaron had actually asked her to go to Sawyers with him. It wasn't like a real date or anything. She knew Liz and Sherri would be furious if they knew she was meeting him.

Christy combed her hair back with her fingers, knowing she looked a total mess. She tried not to care about her looks. They had never bothered her before, not like it did now. The breeze gave her a windblown look anyway, so there wasn't much she could do to improve her hair.

She arrived at Sawyers first. She waited for Aaron to park and join her on the sidewalk. "I forgot to bring you jacket to school from the other night."

"No problem. I haven't needed it. I usually just keep it in the jeep so it's there when I do."

Sawyers was busy as usual with the after-school crowd. After discussing what they wanted, Aaron ordered two club sandwiches and sodas. When their order was ready, they found a quiet corner. Christy took a sip of her soda. She was a little nervous, which caused her to feel tongue-tied.

Aaron didn't seem to be nervous at all. In fact, he was laughing. His blue eyes were twinkling as he bit into his club sandwich.

"Are you finished with your history essay yet?" Christy couldn't think of anything else to say.

"I finished it last night," Aaron answered.

"I love anything to do with history," Christy stated.

"What symbol did you write about?"

"The American flag."

"Really? Me too." He laughed. "I don't know if I did the subject justice."

"I know I haven't yet, but I'm still working on it. Words were hard to come by to express what I wanted to say."

"We may print some of the best ones in the paper," Aaron said.

"Really?"

"Don't look now, but two of your favorite people are on their way over."

Christy looked up, expecting anyone but Liz and Sherri. They were moving across the room, headed straight toward their table. After one look at Liz and Sherri's faces, she could tell they were not pleased to find her with Aaron.

"We didn't think you would be here yet," Sherri complained to Aaron as she took a chair beside him. "The way you talked, we thought you would be with Mr. Coleman forever."

"It didn't take as long as I thought."

It was obvious to Christy that Aaron had planned to meet his friends, and she couldn't help but feel a little disappointed. Both Liz and Sherri had gone home and changed and were wearing new outfits. They looked great while she must appeared a total wreck.

"Christy, you look like you haven't been home since practice," Liz commented not too pleasantly as she flashed Christy one of her phony smiles.

Coming on top of her last thought, Christy really felt uncomfortable. She knew she must have been blushing. Seeing the other two girls gloating about it really didn't help her self-esteem. *Why did she always find herself in these situations?*

"I thought you would be spending all your time practicing so you will be ready for the purple-and-white game next week. We hear the second team thinks they're going to beat us," Sherri said, her eyes shooting daggers at Christy.

"There is always hope," Christy replied, not bothered by the look Sherri gave her.

"Hopes about all you have in your favor," Liz commented with a giggle.

"We'll see," Christy said.

"Christy went to tutoring too," Aaron stated. It was obvious he was trying to change the subject.

"Really," Liz responded. "Let me guess. You were having the same problem as Aaron."

"You know, that is strange," Christy confirmed, setting back in her chair. She had a strong urge to pour the rest of her drink over Liz's head. "We actually were having the same problem. But since we are in the same class, I would say the probability of that occurring would be pretty high."

"Aaron, you know I told you I would help you," Sherri complained. "Why didn't you let me?"

"I have a feeling Mr. Coleman explained it much better than you could." Bill laughed as he brought a tray with his and the girls' orders to the table. "Remember the last time you were going to help me?"

"You do have a way of getting way over our heads when you start talking about all those x's and y's," Liz agreed with Bill.

"Wow, thanks!" Sherri sputtered. "You really know how to make a girl feel good."

"Really, Sherri, I appreciate the offer, but it isn't fair to take up your time on something I didn't get in class," Aaron responded.

"Aaron, you know I wouldn't mind helping you anytime," Sherri replied sweetly.

Christy set her empty soda glass on the table. She had

had enough. She really wasn't in the mood to watch and listen to any more of the girl's flirting.

She stood up to leave. "Thanks for the sandwich," she told Aaron. "I need to go."

"So soon?" Aaron said as he got up too.

"Aaron you can't leave yet. We just got here," Sherri pleaded. "Surely Christy can see herself out?"

"Sherri is right. Finish your food," Christy replied.

"I'll see you tomorrow," Aaron said as he sat back down.

"We haven't had a chance to talk all day," Sherri pouted as Aaron returned to his seat.

"Sorry, Sherri, I've been busy all day," Aaron returned. "Maybe tomorrow will not be as busy."

That was the last Christy heard of the conversation going on at the table she just left. She would not have come if she had known Liz and Sherri were meeting Aaron. On the trip home, she decided she and Aaron could only be friends. It was obvious that he and Sherri must be dating since they were together all the time, and he was meeting her today. *Was he just being friendly, so he asked me to go, or was there another reason?*

*Lord, I am not doing too good in my relationship with Aaron. I keep getting all these mixed signals. Does he like me or not? Is he dating Sherri? Why did he ask me to go to Sawyers if he is dating her? Why does he keep acting like he might like me? I really do like him, so if You could help me here a little, I would really appreciate it. I love You.*

# 17

Liz and Sherri were waiting beside Christy's locker when she arrived in the dressing room for practice the next day. They had given her several fierce looks during the day when they met in the hall and once in the cafeteria while waiting in line for lunch.

"You think you're going to break Aaron and me up!" Sherri declared while flashing her a blistering look.

"I didn't realize the two of you were a couple," Christy responded as she dialed the combination to her lock and tried to remain calm.

"Well, we are. I want you to leave him alone," Sherri demanded.

"I suggest you have this talk with Aaron, not me." There was an exasperated tone in Christy replied.

"We all know you're chasing him, like following him to tutoring!" Liz added backing up her friend.

"I didn't know Aaron was going to be at tutoring yesterday, but I would have gone anyway if I had known,"

Christy declared as she opened her locker and started changing clothes for practice.

"Aaron is mine! You had better leave him alone if you know what's good for you!"

"Does Aaron know this?" Christy responded.

"What do you mean?

"I just assumed if Aaron was yours and he knew that, we wouldn't be having this conversation."

"If you know what is good for you, stay away from him!" Sherri shouted.

"Get this straight Sherri. When Aaron wants me to stop talking to him, he can tell me himself."

"You'll be sorry," Sherri sputtered. "You'll see!"

"See somewhere else," Christy replied as she finished tying her tennis shoes before pushing past Sherri. The second bell rang as she went out the door but she couldn't resist adding, "Don't be too late; you might have to run laps."

Practice was even more frustrating than usual once Liz and Sherri joined them. Liz was again picking on her own teammates. Karri was getting most of the harassment. She was almost in tears before the practice was half over.

Christy didn't understand why Coach Thomas didn't say something. Surely she could see what was going on. Liz was definitely doing this on purpose as once again she was on Karri about a bad pass. The more she said, the more mistakes Karri made. Christy finally had enough. If Coach Thomas wasn't going to say anything she would.

"Liz, that's enough!" Christy shouted.

"She needs to do it right!" Liz shouted back.

"Maybe she would if you'd stop hounding her every move."

"Would you like to make me?" Liz demanded.

"That's enough girls! Rivers, take Taylor's position.

On hearing this, Karri ran off the court in tears.

Christy stared at the Coach for a moment. "I'm going to check on Karri."

Not waiting for a reply, she left the court. There was no way she could pass a ball to Liz right now without bouncing it off her head. *Why couldn't the Coach see what Liz was doing? Didn't she care?*

Karri definitely needed someone to check on her. Christy could hear her sobs all the way from the hallway before she opened the dressing room door.

"Karri? Are you alright?" Christy asked as she approached her.

Karri just cried all the harder.

Christy sat down next to her on the bench. "Don't let Liz upset you so."

"I hate her!" Karri gasp between sobs. "She has ruined my life. I wish I were dead!"

"Karri, don't say things like that." Christy was shocked by what she heard. "Nothing can be that bad."

"But it is!" Karri cried. "My Mom won't let me be friends with you because of all of her lies. I can't stand her threatening me all the time. I just can't!"

"Listen, Karri. We have to talk. Everyone will be in here before long so just change your shoes. You can take your clothes."

"I don't understand why you will even speak to me after what I did to you?"

"Because you're my friend," Christy answered. "Now hurry up before the others get in here."

She changed into her own shoes, and they were on their way out the door when Coach Thomas opened it from the other side. "Is everything all right?"

"Karri just needs someone to talk to about a personnel problem. We are leaving before everyone gets in here."

"Go ahead. I'll keep everyone until the bell rings."

They went to their lockers in the hallway and got their books. When the bell rang, they were getting in Christy's jeep.

Karri lived just a few blocks from school. When they reached her house, Christy drove the jeep under the carport and parked.

"Is your Mom home?" Christy asked.

"No, she is working late today." Karri answered.

"Then you are coming with me. We need to sit down and talk. I don't know what Liz can threaten you with, but it's time you told someone. If you can't tell you mother, I hope you feel you can talk to a friend."

"You still want to be my friend?"

"I've never stopped being your friend, Karri. I don't know of any reason that I wouldn't want to be friends with you."

"You might change your mind when you hear what I have to tell you," Karri said tears again rolling down her cheeks.

"You're coming over to my house. We are going to get this straightened out," Christy said assuring her. "Do you need anything from inside?"

"No," she said.

Christy backed out and drove home in silence. Mary Rivers welcomed Karri when they arrived like nothing out of the ordinary had been going on. She didn't ask any questions, of which Christy was grateful, giving them cookies and soft drinks for a snack before they went upstairs to Christy's room.

Finally Christy was able to ask, "Well, are you going to tell me or not?"

She was seated on the side of her bed while Karri sit in the window seat looking out over the front lawn.

Karri sat with her face turned away from Christy. "You know it was me who lied to Coach Thomas about that night." Karri said grimly.

"Yes, I know," Christy answered. "I forgive you."

"And you still want to be my friend?" Karri said. She couldn't believe it.

"What really happened the night of the party that gave Liz the power to make you lie?" She wished that Karri would tell her what was going on so they could put this all behind them.

"I did something really stupid," Karri replied tears streaming down her face.

"It can't be that terrible."

"It is," Karri responded sadly. "I don't know how to fix it. All the lies have just made everything worse."

"They usually do," Christy stated. "You start out with a small one, but it grows, and the next thing you know…"

"What a mess," Karri whispered. "If it weren't for the pictures, I would think this was all just a bad nightmare."

"Pictures?"

"Liz kept saying pictures don't lie."

"What kind of pictures?"

"They show…well…they show me drinking and taking drugs…" Karri finally got out.

"I heard about the drinking, but I don't believe you took drugs!" Christy declared with total disbelief on her face.

"I saw them, Christy. I kept thinking Liz and Sherri were somehow lying. But I saw the pictures of Barry and me. We both were drinking, and he was giving me some drugs in one picture. I was letting him put pills in my mouth in two different pictures."

"Are you sure?" Christy asked, still not believing what she was hearing.

"What do you mean 'Am I sure?' I saw them. They weren't fakes."

"You know for sure they were of you?"

"It was my face on those pictures," Karri said. "I guess the drugs are the reason I can't remember anything but drinking a beer. I don't recall there being any drugs there… there must have been…I'm just so ashamed."

"That's how they got you to lie to Coach Thomas."

"Yeah," Karri whispered. "I'm sorry about that Christy. I know how important playing ball this year is to you."

"Liz knew that too."

"At first, she was saying she would show the pictures to my mom. You know how much that would hurt her after what happened to my brother. Lately, she has been talking about showing the pictures at school. I'd rather die than for everyone to see those pictures and think I'm like that. I don't know what to do anymore."

"Karri, I think Liz pulled a cruel prank on all of us

that night. I know you heard about us getting stuck that night and the next morning the car not being stuck."

"Yeah, I heard about that, but I also know what happened. It was her brother and some of his fraternity buddies. They pulled the prank for their pledge in a fraternity at college. It seems Liz helped plan the whole thing when she learned her brother and his friends had to do something really outrageous to get in."

"I knew she was involved somehow. The worst part of the whole thing was no one believed us because there was no evidence of us being stuck."

"I'm sorry, Christy, but I couldn't tell you."

"We had an idea Liz was behind this, but why she would go to so much trouble didn't make sense. We decided she had to pay someone to get the car out and clean it up before the next morning. I can see how the whole thing fell right in place. Now I believe even more strongly someone who would plan something out so well could certainly do something even weirder like creating some fake pictures."

"I wish I could believe that," Karri admitted.

"What does Barry say about the pictures?"

"I haven't talked to him since that night," Karri replied. "I just couldn't believe what I had done. I leave whenever Barry comes around."

"I don't think you did anything with drugs."

"But the pictures…"

"Are fakes," Christy said with conviction.

"How?" Karri asked in wonder. The hopeful look on her face indicated how badly she hoped Christy was right.

"There are all kinds of technology out there. I just

hope Liz is as good at taking as she is dishing out," Christy said with an expression on her face that said Liz was in for some of her own medicine. "Come on. I want to show you something, and I have a plan to fix all of this."

*Forgive me Lord for I am about to sin.*

Christy took Karri downstairs to her dad's study. There she turned on the computer, and while she was waiting for it to power up, she took a picture of Karri. After a few more minutes, she turned the picture so Karri could see the computer screen.

"They actually look like the real thing?" Karri said as she looked from one photograph to another with a sense of wonder on her face. "If I hadn't seen what you did, I would think these were original prints."

"This is what I believe Liz and Sherri did to those pictures they showed you," Christy insisted.

"How can you be so sure?" Karri asked. Even seeing evidence, she couldn't help but doubt what her eyes were telling her.

"Because I know you," said Christy loyally. "I believe Anne would have noticed."

Karri smiled through tears. "Thanks for having faith in me. You seem to know me better than I know myself."

"Come on. Let's get out of here," Christy said turning off her Grandmother's computer.

She was so glad her grandmother had shown her this latest program and what you could do with photographs. Technology is wonderful when used correctly, but it shouldn't be used to ruin people's lives.

"How would they be able to do it? Do they have all

the equipment too?" Karri asked, doubt slipping back into her voice.

"Sherri's mother works in advertisement. I'm sure she uses some of the same technology my grandmother uses for magazine articles."

"I know we aren't supposed to want to get revenge, but I want to make them pay for this."

"Getting ourselves in trouble is not the best revenge. In fact, I would say it would be playing right into their hands."

"The best revenge would be her having to share playing first team with you this year," Karri insisted. "That would be great."

"I still can't understand her objections to that."

"She's scared she will no longer be the star on the court."

"She can't think I am going to take away from her playing?"

"She doesn't want someone else upstaging her. Would you believe she went to three basketball camps this past summer so she could get even better? She is really weird on this."

"She doesn't have anything to worry about from me. I wish she would only see how good our team could be if we all worked together."

"She is selfish, and she likes things the way they are." Karri added. "What I want to know is what are we going to do to combat this. You and I both know anyone who went to this much trouble isn't going to just roll over and not retaliate if we strike back."

"Oh, I thought we might come up with something

that would prevent the pictures being used against you," Christy said. A gleam in her eyes that spoke of mischief to come. "Sometimes you have to face bullies. They leave you no other choice."

"How?"

"You're going to do a presentation to the class on this newest technology. The only thing we need is some pictures of Liz, Sherri and Barry, which I think we can get tomorrow. The other thing is you have to act as if nothing has changed where Liz and Sherri won't know we have found them out. They have to continue to think they have the upper hand."

"I guess I can continue this for a little longer if it will keep them from using those pictures," Karri said. "How do we get the pictures?"

"I think I can cover that."

Karri laughed for the first time in days. "I have a feeling this is going to be good, and I can't wait to see their faces."

"Just remember you have to continue to act as if they could ruin your life at any time."

"Don't worry. I'm not going to do anything that might jeopardize getting out of this mess. Please remind me, if I ever want to go anywhere near anything they have going on, to run the other way."

"Believe me, I'll be right behind you," Christy hugged her friend. "I've really missed you."

"I know. Me too."

"Come on. I'll call Bobby to come and get you. Hopefully they will never know you have been here."

When Karri left, Christy went to her room and picked

up the phone. She dialed a number and waited for the call to go through. A moment later she heard a familiar voice on the other end say, "Hello."

"Aaron, this is Christy. I need a favor."

"Sure, if I can."

"I need you to take some pictures for me at school tomorrow. Since you already take them for the paper, no one will think anything about it."

"I'd be glad to take some pictures of you."

"Oh, it's not me I need pictures of."

"Then who?"

"Liz, Sherri and Barry." Christy replied.

There was complete silence on the other end of the line for a long pause. Aaron finally said, "Why do I get the feeling you are up to something here?"

"I can't explain right now. But you know they would never let me take pictures of them."

"This has to be done tomorrow?"

"The sooner the better," Christy answered. "And Aaron?"

"Yes."

"No one can know you're taking the pictures for me, and I mean no one."

"Just so no one will suspect anything, do you want me to take pictures of other people too?" Aaron asked from the other end of the line.

"You know, that is definitely a good idea."

"Glad you agree."

"Thanks, Aaron. I'll owe you one."

"I'm keeping tabs," Aaron laughed. "I'll let you know when I'm ready to collect."

*Please, Lord, let this work. I don't plan to use evil to get even, I just plan to use some of the same medicine to take care of the problem that is causing Karri pain. Please forgive me and let this work. I Love You.*

# 18

The next day Christy thought Karri deserved an Oscar for her performance. She acted as if she didn't know Christy and Anne when they met in the hall. She still kept the look of unhappiness on her face, and it was obvious Liz and Sherri didn't suspect anything.

Aaron took pictures around the campus all day. At lunch Christy watched him take several pictures of Liz, Sherri and Barry. Liz and Sherri had even talked him into being in a picture with them, and they asked Karri to take the picture. Karri had tried to get out of it, saying she might mess something up.

Liz laughed and said, "Anyone can point a camera and push a button."

Bill appeared out of nowhere to be in the picture, and Karri had taken a picture of the four friends.

Christy couldn't help but wonder if she was being unfair to Aaron. These were his friends. *How would he feel when he learned that his pictures were going to be used to teach them a lesson?* She couldn't tell him until after the deed was done. *Would he still want to be her friend when he learned the truth?* One look at Karri's face, she knew she had no other choice. Liz had started this, and she would help her friend even if she lost a friendship she really would like to keep.

As they dressed for basketball practice, it was plain Liz and Sherri had no idea that anything was going on. Liz took it a little easier on everyone for a change, making Christy wonder if Coach Thomas may have spoken to her. There was no repeat of the day before.

On the surface, everything seemed normal, but beneath, Christy knew it was only a matter of time before Liz's hold on Karri would no longer exist. She could hardly wait because by this time tomorrow, Liz would not be able to blackmail her friend.

Coach Thomas blew her whistle, a shrill shriek that got everyone's attention. She waited until all the girls had gathered around her before motioning for them to have a seat on the floor.

"There are less than seven scrimmage days until the purple-and-white game. A week after that, we will open the season with the Crossett Eagles here. I feel we are in fair shape, but I want you to know that there is still too much friction on this team for it to be where it could be. I hope some of you will take some time and consider what you need to do to leave your disagreements somewhere else for what is better for the team."

"I've posted the teams for the purple-and-white game on the bulletin board. We will spend the rest of the time in practice between now and next Friday getting ready.

Each team will practice on opposite ends of the court during practice time, but can also schedule times outside of practice if you would like to. You need to select a caption once you see which team, you're on. The captain will be in charge of organizing the practices and game plans. Any questions?" She paused a minute. "Check on your team and get to work."

Players went to the corridor where the bulletin board was outside the locker room. They looked to see where their names were on the two pieces of paper thumb-tacked to the bulletin board. Christy wasn't surprised to find her name listed on the purple team. The other players were busy looking for their own names or their friends. Anne, Mia and Tonya were all listed on the purple team. The biggest surprise was that Karri's name was on their team's list near the bottom.

"Coach Thomas, is there some mistake about Karri being on the purple team?" Liz asked as Coach Thomas walked up to where the girls stood.

"No, Liz, I don't think so. Do you have a problem with it?"

Liz seemed speechless at first. "No, of course not," she finally replied. The look she gave Christy as she was walking away to join her group said otherwise.

Christy's team quickly selected her to be the captain. They agreed to try and practice two or three time off campus at the city park before they were to play the purple-and-white game.

Once the teams took the court, the practice whirled by. Coach Thomas spent part of the class period practicing with each group. Christy felt fairly happy with how things were going. When Coach Thomas dismissed them for the day, she asks her group to stay a few minutes so they could discuss meeting for extra practices. She really didn't want to be in the locker room with Liz and Sherri because she knew Liz was pretty mad about how the teams had been divided up. This also kept Karri away from Liz.

*Thank You, Lord, for today's surprise. Things are looking up.*

Mia was smiling from ear to ear as she said, "I can't believe we are going to get to play on the same team. We are going to beat Liz and her team."

"Me either," Tonya laughed. "Christy, you must have been praying for this miracle."

"Not exactly, but Karri is on our team is a nice surprise." Christy replied.

"Glad to be on your side again," Karri said with tears in her eyes. "It's not much fun being on Liz's team."

"Can all of you be at the park Thursday after school around four?" Christy asked.

"What about tomorrow?" Mia asked.

"I have church on Wednesdays," Christy replied.

"Yeah, me too," Anne said.

"Thursday it is," Tonya agreed. "Come on, Mia. Let's get changed. My mom will be waiting on us."

The rest of the girls headed to the dressing room to get ready to go home. Christy was glad to see most of the players had already changed and left the locker room. Mostly she was glad Liz and Sherri were not in sight, and they were able to change and be on their way without a run-in with the two.

"Tomorrow is a big day for you, Karri. Are you ready

to go work on your presentation?" Christy questioned Karri as they left the building together.

"What about the pictures?" Karri said.

"Aaron is sending them by email." Christy walked around her jeep to get in while Karri opened the door on the passenger side.

"I can't thank you enough for all you did for me, Christy," Karri told her tears again close to the surface.

"You would have done the same for me."

Karri took a few seconds to answer. "I want to think I would, Christy, but look what I did. I let you down. It's hard to forgive myself for that."

"Put it behind you. After all, think of how much Jesus forgave us for our sins. How could I not forgive you."

Ten minutes later, they pulled into Christy's drive. Christy was ready to check on the pictures that Aaron was sending by email. She could hardly wait to use technology to fix Karri's problems so Liz and Sherri would no longer have any leverage over her.

*Thank You, Lord. Please let the pictures work and forgive us where we have failed You.*

The sounds of laughter meet Christy as she stepped into the school hallway the next morning. Students were standing around in groups pointing and laughing at pictures displayed up and down the hallways. It was obvious their plan just might work.

"What's going on?" Christy asked as if she didn't have a clue as she reached the first group of students.

"Can you believe these pictures?" responded one of the students.

"Aren't they neat?" someone else replied.

"Come here, Christy! You just have to see this one!" Tonya pointed at one of the pictures.

Christy couldn't help but laugh when she saw the picture everyone found so ridiculous. It was one of her leaping into the air and dunking a basketball.

"I wish I could do that." Christy laughed.

"These are really awesome," someone behind them commented.

"We're sure to find out about this in science today," Christy stated before she walked back outside.

She was smiling when she exited the building. Everyone outside was talking about the pictures, and one look at Liz and Sherri with their head together was enough for her to know they had seen the images on display.

"Did you see the pictures on display in the hall?" Anne asked, as Christy joined their group.

"They are really something." Christy commented.

"I guess you're use to that kind of technology with your grandmother working on publishing of magazine articles," Anne said.

"She doesn't change pictures, but the technology is there to make them clear and more appealing. It is really something what you can do today with technology." Christy answered.

"I am sure we are going to hear about it in science today." Anne commented.

"Did you see the one of you and Liz with your arms around each other's shoulders?" Aaron asked as he walked up behind them. "I had to look twice before I would believe my eyes."

"Just goes to show you can't believe everything you see," Christy told him when she noticed he wasn't smiling. "I hope you will forgive me for involving you." She said it quietly so no one else would overhear them.

"I'm sure you are going to tell me what this is all about."

"I can't right at this moment. But I promise I will fill you in if you have a little time after school," Christy stated just as the bell rung.

"Saved by the bell," Aaron said as they turned to go to their first class of the day.

"Aaron, why on earth would you ruin our picture and put Christy in it?" Christy heard Liz complaining to Aaron as everyone moved down the hallway.

"The point was to take something that was believable making it into something unbelievable. That I think was accomplished. But I only took the pictures. Someone else did the artwork," said Aaron, walking away.

Later in the day, Karri was standing with Mrs. Craig in her doorway as students passed into the classroom. Christy was glad she was present to witness the look on Liz and Sherri's faces when they realized Karri was responsible for the pictures in the hallway. It was even funnier when Karri finished presenting her project by informing the class that she couldn't take full credit for the idea for this project alone.

"Mrs. Craig, I think I should give Liz and Sherri special recognition for showing me some artwork that they had been doing with computer and camera. This is where the idea came from, so if you enjoyed this project, I hope you will be sure and tell them."

"That is very kind of you to want to include your friends," Mrs. Craig said. "I am expecting them to do their own projects. Class, you can now have a chance to look closer at the pictures and ask Karri about anything that interest you about her project."

"You're the one that is responsible for all of this?" Liz hissed. "We thought Aaron was."

"Actually, I could give you full credit for all of this." Karri quietly replied. "Not only was this your idea but the idea, but the idea that the pictures needed to be fakes were yours also. You should see some of the pictures I now have that are fakes that I didn't display. But then you might not appreciate them too much, just as I didn't care too much for the ones you showed me. I'm sure I can be persuaded to keep them under lock and key. Isn't that the words you used?"

"You think you're so smart," Liz hissed under her breath. "This isn't over."

"It had better be. If you ever threaten me again, I will embarrass you and your friends so badly that you'll wish you had never thought up this little charade. And that's not a threat. That's a promise!"

Liz laughed. "Don't worry. We were beginning to get tired of having you underfoot all the time anyway. You served your purpose. Besides it was fun watching you sweat. I will have to hand it to you. I didn't think you were smart enough to figure this one out all by yourself."

"Maybe I didn't do it all by myself."

"I guess you're talking about Little Miss Perfect over there?" Liz hissed

"Her name is Christy." Karri replied. "She is what a true friend is. Something I am sure you will never know anything about."

After class there was no doubt that the pictures had been a true success with the whole school. Aaron came and took a picture for the school newspaper that would be put in the local paper on the project. Several students asked Karri if she would make some special pictures for them.

They were even surprised later in the day when Coach Thomas came into the dressing room after their practice.

She commented on what a great job Karri had done on the project and told her that she wanted her to make up some flyers for the purple-and-white game.

"You think you've won!" Liz said to Christy when Coach Thomas left. "But you haven't!"

"Why does everything have to be a competition with you?" Christy asked. "Don't you see what you're doing to our team with all of this? Don't you even care?"

"I care that the white team beats you next week!"

"What if you don't?" Tonya replied. "What if we beat you?"

"That's not going to happen." Sherri answered. "You're not good enough."

"You might just be surprised how good we are," Mia added.

"If you're that good, you won't be afraid to make a little wager?" Liz grinned.

Christy could tell that this was where Liz had been headed all along. "What do you want Liz?"

"You off the team." Liz replied bitterly.

"Go on." Christy said.

"I've thought of a way I might accept you on the team."

"That is?"

"If the purple team just happened to beat us next week, I might consider you good enough to play with us."

"You're saying if the purple team wins, you would accept me and we can play as teammates?" Christy repeated.

"That's correct."

"Tells us the rest of your plan." Anne said, not believing Liz would be so bold in front of the whole team.

"Oh, you mean the part about if we beat you." Liz laughed. "Haven't y'all figured that out yet? It's simple, Christy gets to go back to being our manager."

"I don't understand you. You're one of the best players on this team. I don't see what difference it makes if I'm on the team or not?" Christy said sadly. "I work just as hard as you, maybe harder, to be a part of this team."

"I am the best player on this team," Liz snapped. "You can't just come in here and steal the show."

"You're not the whole team, Liz." Tonya commented.

"Accept the wager. Either way, the team wins," Liz taunted.

"No, Christy!" Karri shouted.

"Christy don't," Anne added. "This is what she wants."

"You know you want to do what is best for the team," Liz taunted.

"Don't listen to her, Christy," Tonya joined.

"Afraid you'll lose?" Liz asked.

"Can't you see the team is going to be the losers if we don't find a way to work together?" Christy asked.

"Then accept the wager."

"Okay, on one condition," Christy finally replied.

"That is?"

"If we win and you don't live up to your part of the deal, you're the one who has to quit."

Liz laughed. "You've got yourself a deal. Because there is just no way you are going to beat us!"

Christy left the dressing room because she couldn't believe she had just made a wager with Liz that could end her chance to play basketball. This time it was for the team she kept telling herself, but she knew in her heart that she let herself down because this was not what God would have wanted her to do.

*I know You are disappointed with me, Lord. There should have been a better way. Please forgive me because I know I have let You down and along the way myself. If we lose, it is my own fault I will be off the team. I love You*

# 20

Aaron was waiting for Christy beside her jeep when she reached it after school. She was trying hard not to cry, but tears escaped as she drew near where he leaned against it. She knew her expression must look like a storm cloud before a storm, and all she could think of was all the hours spent practicing for a place on the team and now it could all be for nothing.

"What's wrong?" he asked with concern in his voice.

"Just mad at myself," she replied, her mouth a straight line. "I just agreed to something that I know I shouldn't have been a party to."

"Want to talk about it?" He noticed the anger in her eyes seem to have softened.

"It's something I need to pray about, but thanks for the offer," she said. "I did promise you the story about the pictures if you have time."

"I have the afternoon off, and I have something I would like to talk to you about."

"Would you like to come over to my house? I have to practice free throws, but I can fill you in while I do that."

Aaron smiled and motioned with his hand. "Lead the way, I will be right behind you."

After getting in the jeep, Christy reached over and got out one of her favorite Christian disk to listen to on her way home. She cranked the jeep and pulled out as she saw Aaron getting in his. She let the music flow over her and felt some of her anger with herself fading away. Most people would be concerned with what others thought about what had taken place in the locker room. Christy was more concerned with what God thought about what she had let happen. *Would it hurt my Christian testimony with some of the other girls?*

*Consider it joy whenever you face trials knowing that the testing builds perseverance.*

The thought was like a soft whisper to her trouble mind, assuring her God was still in control.

Pulling into the garage when she arrived home, she got out and waited on Aaron to park and join her. He followed her inside through the garage door. Her mother was at the kitchen table with her laptop when they entered the room.

"Hey, Christy," she said, looking a little surprised at the young man following her daughter through the door.

"Mom, this is Aaron Smith. He brought me home the other night when I was stranded at the deer camp."

"Thanks, Aaron, for getting Christy home. Both her father and I are thankful you were there to help her."

"Aaron, this is my mom," Christy told him as he stepped up to greet her.

"Nice to meet you, ma'am," he said shaking her hand. "Glad I was able to help."

"We're going to practice a little shooting." Christy turned to see Aaron right behind her as she went out the door to the basketball court.

Taking a basketball from a basket by the backdoor, she headed for the free throw line. As she took her first shot, Aaron moved to catch the ball as it dropped through the net. Passing it back to her, she continued to shoot and hit each shot up to nineteen before finally missing one.

"You're pretty good," Aaron said as he passed the ball back to her.

Instead of shooting again, Christy moved over to the patio chairs and took a seat. "I promised to tell you the story behind the pictures."

"That's not necessary. I overheard Liz and Sherri talking to Bill. I know the two of them took some pictures of Karri and Barry on the night of the party. They doctored the pictures to make it look like Karri did something that she didn't do. Not sure what that was. Unfortunately, Karri believed them, and I know you needed the pictures I took yesterday to undo what they started."

"Thank you for your help with the pictures,"

"I am glad you were able to use them to defuse the situation for your friend."

"They did the trick, and good came from it." She sighed, deciding not to gossip about it.

"Then, you did good," He added with a smile on his face.

"Actually we did good." She smiled for the first time

that afternoon. "Without your help, Karri would still have this hanging over her."

"Christy, you always have such a positive attitude. Today is the first time I have seen you really down about anything. I have been drawn to you since the first time I saw you on that stage this summer. I heard you speak about God, and your prayer for our country was so sincere. Something happened to me that night. I don't know how to explain it. Something pulls me to want to know more about this God you speak about. At first I tried to fight against it. I know you remember what I said that day at the post office. Little by little, the example you have set has changed my mind about God."

"That's wonderful, Aaron," Christy said as her heart felt happy to know he wanted to know more."

"That night at your house, when all of you sang and praised God. I found myself wanting to have more of what you have. After the first meeting on campus, I've been reading my *Bible,* and I even started with the gospel of John like you recommended," he said with a smile. "I've been listening to some Christian music. I loved that song all of you sang 'Blessed Redeemer.' I later printed out the lyrics and have read it every day since. As I read the accounts in the *Bible,* I keep asking myself, why would Jesus do it?"

"Because He loves us."

"I want to accept Jesus as my Savior, Christy. You led me to Christ. Can you help me with what to say?"

"Do you realize that you are a sinner?" Christy said, wanting to shout for joy that her friend wanted to accept Jesus as his Savior. "The *Bible* says in Romans 3:23 all have sinned and come short of the glory of God. Then, Romans 5:8 says that God showed his love for all men by allowing Jesus to die for them. You see, you are already there. Aaron, all that is left is for you to do is confess you are a sinner and tell Jesus you want Him to come into your heart." Christy laughed as tears flowed down her face. "Romans 10:13 says for all who call on the name of the Lord shall be saved."

"I memorized John 3:16. God loved the world so much that He gave His only begotten Son, that whosoever believeth in Him should not perish but have everlasting life," Aaron told her. "I believe in God, but I'm not sure how to talk to Him."

"You are not going to disappoint God. There is no magical prayer. Just truly tell Him your feelings and let Him know you want Him to come into your heart."

"Okay, here goes. Lord, I'm not sure what all I need to say for you to save me, but I am confessing that I am a sinner and that I want You to forgive me. I want You to be a part of my life. Thank you for loving me enough to die on a cross so I can have eternal life. There is so much I want to learn. I just need your help. Thank You for my new friends. Amen"

When he finished and looked up, Christy hugged him and said, "Welcome to the family of God. You are now my brother in Christ, a child of the King."

"I'm saved," he responded with a big smile on his face. "Thank you, Christy. I am going home to tell my family, so I will see you later at church. I can't wait to tell Brother Joe."

# 21

By game time on Friday night, electricity was in the air as the referee blew his whistle to indicate the start of the purple-and-white game. Christy and her teammates clasped hands and pumped once and shouted in unison, "Let's win!"

They broke their circle, and Christy, Anne, Tonya, Mia and Karri ran onto the court to take up their positions. The rest of the purple team sat down to watch the beginning of the game.

All that was left was the game to be played. Christy felt her teammates were as ready as they would ever be. In the week leading up to the game, every free moment had been spent getting ready for this game. After the day of the wager, both teams had set to work, practicing beating the other. There were no other incidents during school. Both teams had decided the outcome would be finished on the playing court.

Liz and Tonya jumped at center court. Tonya out

jumped Liz by several inches and tipped the ball to Christy, who quickly set up the play and begin moving the ball up the court. Liz and Sherri both signed their players back on defense. Christy passed the ball to Anne, who faked her guard out and drove into the paint. When she was cut off, she passed back out to Christy. She caught the pass and drove into the middle of the paint.

Liz had to move over to pick her up, and she bounced-passed to Tonya, who put up a jump shot that Liz was unable to block. The first two points of the game were on the board. The first play came easy, unfortunately the rest of the period was a lot of fast action with both teams up and down the court. Nervousness was forgotten as they played to defeat each other. The purple team led twelve to ten at the end of the first period.

"Just stay cool," Christy cautioned her team. "We are doing okay, but we have to keep the ball out of Liz's hands as much as possible. Remember our strategies coming into this game. We can do this."

The girls joined hands and again pumped once, shouting, "Let's Win!" before running back onto the court for the beginning of the second-quarter play.

The second quarter went much as the first period, the main difference was the purple team used their whole bench and kept fresh players in the game.

Liz was playing well. In fact she had never been in better form, and it was obvious she was playing to win. Both teams were playing to the best of their abilities, and it was apparent the Lady Lions, should they get their team to play together, were going to have a great year. Christy and Tonya both had made steals at the beginning of the second quarter that led to scores. Still by the end of the first half, Liz's team had come back and was up twenty-six to twenty-two.

The purple team was making a tremendous effort to win, and Christy felt so proud of each of them. She knew each of them was playing their hearts out to keep her on the team. She felt a lump in her throat. They deserved to win, but as the third period turned into the last minutes of the fourth period the white team continued to hold the lead by four points. Each time the purple team scored, the white team had managed to come back with an answer.

Time was running out. They had taken advantage of Christy and Tonya being the main shooters and had double-teamed them every time down the court. With a minute to go, Christy had knocked down a three-pointer to bring the score to forty-eight to forty-seven, a one-point game. Liz's team had brought the ball down the court, and was stalling, trying to run the clock out. With fifteen seconds left on the clock, Karri stole a bounce pass intended for Sherri. She quickly called a time-out.

They formed a circle around Christy, waiting to see what their last play for the game would be.

"You already know what to do, and I want you to know that, win or lose, right now, I couldn't be any happier about a game than I am about this one. You're all a special group of friends, and no matter what the final score is, we're winners just for having had this chance to play together as a team."

"Christy, you sound like you don't think we are going to win this one," Tonya said. "You know our winner's creed. We can do this! We are going to do this!"

"Let's go show Liz she's not getting her way this time," Karri added. "We are winning this one!"

"Yeah! Let's win!" Tonya and Mia shouted together.

One last time they joined hands for their cry, "Let's Win!"

They threw the ball into Karri, who dribbled once and passed to Mia, who dribbled up the court. Christy and Tonya were both running crossing patterns at the other end of the court under the goal. Anne broke across the center court and caught a pass from Mia. Then immediately passed back to Karri, who had broken toward the top of the key.

Karri caught the ball and dribbled once, stopping just inside the paint. She put up a jump shot that no one had come out to cover. The ball left her hand and arched toward the goal before dropping through with a soft swish just as the final buzzer sounded.

The noise was tremendous as the whole team raced toward Karri. Christy reached her first and hugged her before Tonya picked her up and swung her around. The rest of the team was hugging, jumping, and screaming. One would have thought they had just won a state championship. Instead, they had just made a play work that they had worked on for a whole week just in case they found themselves in such a position. They had banked on the white team thinking Tonya or Christy would take the last shot. Instead, they had planned all along for Karri to be the one to take it. Their strategy had worked.

The purple team finally stopped celebrating long enough to shake hands with the players on the white team. Liz and Sherri had already headed to the dressing room.

The other players hugged both girls and told them they had played a great game.

"We're going to be awesome this year."

The thought troubled Christy as she walked toward the dressing room with a feeling of apprehension. *Our year would depend on Liz. How is she going to react to losing? Everyone knew she didn't like to lose.* The Lady Lions needed Liz just as badly as they needed Christy. Working together was the only way that they would ever be true winners.

Once through the dressing room doors, the happy smiles vanished off the faces of the players. Liz was sitting alone on a bench in front of the lockers. She starred straight at Christy as she entered the room. Sherri wasn't in sight. Everyone seemed to have deserted her. This was the first time Christy could ever remember Liz being alone without a group surrounding her.

"Aren't you going to gloat?" Liz asked.

"You played a great game, Liz," Christy replied. "If we went back out and played another quarter the result would probably be the other way around."

"You're always, Little Miss Perfect," Liz stated bitterly. "Isn't it enough you won?"

"That's just it, Liz, I individually didn't win. The purple team won. Basketball is a team sport. You of all people should know that, and each member of the team has to contribute to be winners.  That's what we did. We played as a team and won as a team."

"You always have an answer for everything," Liz complained.

"We have an individual star with you on our team, but that doesn't make us a team. And certainly, doesn't make us a winning team." Christy waited to see how Liz would respond.

"I don't even like you!" Liz replied. So, why would I want to play basketball with you?"

"Because you like to win," Christy returned. "You're forgetting how great it feels, and together that is what we can do. We can win."

"Come on, Liz," one of the other girls said. "You know she's right. Surely even you know that with Christy on the team, she makes you a better player. The rest of us have seen it even if you haven't."

"A deal is a deal," Tonya added.

"What if I decide not to honor my side of the deal?" Liz asked.

"Then you are a fool, Liz." Mai said from behind her. "You worked so hard to get Christy to agree to this deal that you never considered you might be the one to lose. Well, you did, and if you don't honor your part of the deal, I don't think there will be enough players left on this team for you to play either."

"You're saying that you won't play if Christy doesn't play?" Liz asked looking stunned.

"That's what most of us are saying," Anne replied. "Which will it be, Liz? A winning year, or no year at all?"

"Okay! I hear you," Liz finally said. "I may not like it, but I will try."

"Yeah!" several of the players shouted together. "Before this year is over, you're going to be glad that you made that decision. You just wait and see."

Christy knew it took a lot for Liz to accept her on the team. When she put her hand out, Liz reluctantly shook it. Then all the other players begin clapping. The feud seems to be over. Christy knew with Liz you could never tell, but once they started playing as a team, maybe Liz would see they were right.

"We have a chance of going to state this year Liz." Christy stated.

"You know, with a stubborn little package like you on our team, we probably will." Liz commented without smiling.

"One step at a time!" Christy laughed.

"Yeah!" Liz finally smiled. "By the way, you did play a pretty good game."

"What would life be without a few surprises thrown in?"

"Dull!" Tonya shouted. "Just plain dull!"

"Let's get changed so we can watch the boys' game," Anne said. "I want to see my brother play. By the way are we going to Sawyers after the game?"

Everyone hurried to get changed. The noise grew steadily louder as Christy, Anne, Karri, Tonya and Mia left the dressing room together. Parents were cheering for their children. Due to all the noise, she almost didn't hear her name being called.

Turning, she saw Aaron standing near the door of the dressing room she had just come out of. He was leaning against the wall with his arms crossed over his chest. It took a moment for it to register who stood there beside him. She couldn't believe her eyes. For there stood her parents and Sam.

"Dad! Sam!" She cried and took off toward them.

Once her father's arms were around her, she burst into

tears, and she couldn't stop crying. They were happy tears, and then she felt Sam joining into a group hug. She didn't want to let either one of them go, and they stood there for several moments before Christy was finally able to pull back and look up into her father's and brother's faces.

"You're really here! I'm not dreaming?" She got out past the lump in her throat.

There were people clapping and yelling all around them, but they seemed happy to just hold on to each other for a while.

"Couldn't believe my eyes when I saw you playing out there on the purple team, sis." Sam told her as he hugged her one more time. "You're shooting was amazing."

"You were here during the game?" She questioned, not believing she didn't know they were in the stands."

"Yes, we were," her father said. "I must say your mother told me you were coming along just fine, but I wasn't expecting to see you play like that."

"Way to go, girls!" several people said from the crowded hallway.

Lots of people were shaking her father's and Sam's hands as they passed by.

"Thanks," they all said in unison.

"You beat all, Christy Rivers." Aaron's laughing voice made her look up. Her heartbeat increased at what she saw in his blue eyes as he stared back.

She blushed. "Is that good or bad?" The smile on her face said it didn't matter right now. All was well with her life.

"Oh, definitely good," he replied as he reached for her

hand. "You played a wonderful game. The way the team worked together was really inspiring."

"We were a team." Christy admitted as she looked around at the rest of her team members who were all grinning back at her.

"I look forward to watching you play this year," he added, obviously encouraged by the fact that she didn't pull her hand away.  "Would you mind if I sit with you and your family for the boys' game."

"You don't have to take pictures?" Christy asked.

"Barry's taking pictures tonight. I'm getting to watch for a change."

Christy smiled up at him, unaware of the effect she was having on him. "Then I would love for you to watch the game with us."

"Are you ready to find a seat in the stands," she asked her father.

"Lead the way," he replied as he smiled at his daughter and the boy who still held her hand in his.

Aaron held on to her hand as he guided them to seats in the stands. "I accidentally saw some news that will be in Tuesday's paper. The Arkansas Unit that your dad is with will not to be reactivated again anytime in the near future."

"Are you sure," she cried.

"If it is being put in the paper, it came down through dependable channels."

"I could kiss you." She laughed.

*No one knew how happy that makes me that my father and brother would be staying on American soil. Thank You, Lord.*

"I wouldn't object, but I don't think we had better do that in this crowd. Especially, since we are on the school campus and I think your dad might not care for some guy he doesn't know to be kissing on his daughter." He laughed. "You can always remind me later by singing that song about are you going to kiss me or not." The mischief look in his eyes had her smiling as they went to search out seats in the stands.

She couldn't stop grinning as she said, "I happened to know the words to that song."

Holding hands with Aaron as he guided her up the steps to where the rest of her friends were seated in the bleachers seemed almost like a dream. The knowing looks on her friends' faces told her she was very awake and let her know they would pick on her later, but not in front of Aaron.

Sam sat down on her other side, and her father and mother took a seat behind them. She leaned back and could touch her father's knees. Just knowing he was home to stay filled her with pure joy and made her want to shout, "*Thank You, Lord, I feel so very blessed,*" from the rafters.

"By the way, Barry really likes Karri," Aaron said during a time-out a short time later. "Do you think there is any chance she might give him another chance?"

"We could always ask her," Christy replied with a big smile on her face.

"Maybe we could invite them to go on a date with us?" he asked softly.

There was a promise in Aaron's eyes as he smiled at her. *So this was what it felt like to have someone special like you that you felt the same about.* She couldn't believe the day was turning out to be one of the happiest days of her life. She could hardly wait to experience the next step of what life had in store. One thing for sure, her winner's creed would be a part of that future.